URBAN
Pulp Fiction

PHOENIX JAMES

Books may be purchased by contacting: phoenixjamesbooks@gmail.com

Cover Design: KreationsK
Interior Design: KreationsK
Published by: Phoenix James
Editor: Urban Diamond Publishing

Contributing author: R.C Montgomery- Chapter 8

ISBN: 978-0-578-67937-2
         978-0-578-67936-5

Printed in United States

CHAPTER ONE
Stepping Out

Buzz, buzz, buzz, buzz.

Phoenix removed the covers from her face and glanced over her shoulder at her alarm clock.

10 am. Shit. Here we go again.

Phoenix rolled over to her back, stretching her long athletic body. She had a lot to do before her 11 pm shift at the club. She stared at the ceiling, trying to mentally prepare herself for the day. The small cracks in the plaster started to form shapes. Her mind began to drift off, and she could make out what looked like a woman's face and money signs.

"Phee!" Bellowed an all too familiar and hateful voice. Her concentration was broken and the images lost.

"Ma'am?" Phoenix hollered back. There was a pause. "Ma'am?" Phoenix rolled her eyes. She'd been living with the woman most of her childhood, she knew the silence meant, 'Come here now.' Phoenix took in a deep breath then yelled back. "Coming!"

1

She slowly sat up on the edge of the bed. Leaning over, she felt under it with her right hand, in search of her fluffy pink house shoes. She hated those house shoes. The woman of the house, her grandmother Margaret, was old school. Margaret thought bare feet on the floor would give you pneumonia. Hell, going by what Margaret said everything gave you pneumonia. Taking showers in the morning will give you pneumonia, low cut tops gave you pneumonia in the titty. Since Phoenix hated to hear her mouth, she would put them on.

She kneeled down on her brown carpeted bedroom floor, needing a better view of under her bed.Hidden behind her orange and white Nike shoes were her house shoes. She quickly grabbed them. She turned them upside down and tapped them on the floor three times. This was a habit Phoenix had as long as she could remember. Her fear was a spider might be in there. She slid her newly self-pedicured toes into them and shuffled down the hallway into the kitchen.

The smell of fresh-baked biscuits, bacon, eggs, cheese grits, and Maxwell coffee filled the air. Phoenix's stomach growled.

"Ma'am?" Phoenix said a little louder while wiping sleep from her almond-shaped brown eyes. Her grandmother sat at the table. A tall, slender, chocolate-skinned woman well into her late sixties, her hair tied in curls with paper from a brown bag.

Country as hell...take your cheap ass to Wal-Mart and buy some real damn rollers.

Phoenix had years of bottled-up anger against her grandmother. From the moment she came to live with them, Margaret hated her. She would stare at Phoenix with hate in her eyes.

"I should slice your face and see how he treats you then!" She used to threaten. She was jealous of how much attention her grandfather Wolf gave her. Phoenix's back would tighten when Margaret got close to her, afraid one day she might.

With an icy gaze aimed at Phoenix, the older woman sitting at the table sipped her fresh brewed coffee. After a moment Margaret broke the eye contact and her eyes drifted to the sink.

"What's that?"

Phoenix followed her gaze to a double sink full of dirty dishes. "What the hell? I washed dishes last night!" she let out a heavy breath of frustration.

With her full lips pursed and one eyebrow raised her grandmother hissed "I can't tell." She stood up and walked to the sink. "You stop being so damn slick mouthed and lazy you might can get something done." The woman's fussing was interrupted by a loud cackle-like laugh coming down the hallway.

Miesha and Keyonnia, Phoenix's cousins, burst their way into the kitchen. The smell of breakfast was quickly replaced by the unpleasant smell of summer's eve and cheap dollar store perfume. Her cousins were as ratchet as they came. There was no way, Phoenix thought, they shared the same blood.

Keyonnia laughed "Girrrl, I know that nigga burnin'!" She plopped her 5'9, 205 lbs. frame into the wooden kitchen chair. It creaked under the added weight. Keyonnia rubbed her feet together, and they were in desperate need of lotion.

"But you don't know which one gave it to you?" Miesha asked.

"Nope," Keyonnia shot back.

Miesha walked to the kitchen drawer and grabbed a pair of scissors. Keyonnia smirked. Her left fake eyelash was one breath away from falling off.

"I ain't saying shit. I'll wait till they start burnin' and say something to me... shit, I'm playing dumb as hell!" She sat still while Miesha cut the thread from her hair.

Phoenix started to scrape leftover food into an old plastic shopping bag. She shot her cousins a look over her shoulder.

"Can y'all not do that at the table? Hair is getting everywhere." The edge of her lip curled in disgust.

Keyonnia rolled her eyes "Nope!" She turned back to Miesha, "Like I was saying before I was rudely interrupted.... I ain't telling on myself. So, I ain'tneo-soul saying nothing till one of dem say it."Phoenix watched as white dandruff flakes dropped on the table. A shiver went up her spine.

Miesha stepped back and pointed her long Barbie pink stiletto nail. "That's smart! That way you don't snitch on yourself." They high fived each other and laughed again. Phoenix rolled her eyes.

Keyonnia smacked her lips. "Girl! How about Doc gave me $25 to get my hair did and I'm seeing Frank tonight, my paymaster!" Miesha stomped her bare size 12 foot. "Shut up!"

Keyonnia shook her head yes. "All I gotta do is lay there naked while he rubs my ass and jack off. Easy hundred dollars!"

"Damn girl you be lickin'! That's a quick $125 and you didn't have to do shit!" Miesha was impressed.

Phoenix scrubbed the dishes harder. The amount of stupidity coming from them was amazing. Phoenix wondered how could they be only 3 and 4 years apart from her, but at 21 she had more sense than the two of them put together.

5

"Oh shit! I left the pack of hair in my room." Miesha shuffled back to her room.

For the life of her she never picked up her feet. Upon her return, she had in hand four cups, two bowls and three plates. She smiled at Phoenix as she put them in the sink. Phoenix's eyes narrowed. She bit her bottom lip to fight back the word bitch.

"Ooh! Girl let me tell you!" Miesha spit out while tapping Keyonnia on the shoulder. "You know who, said last night while he had me bent over the hood of his car in the back Wal-Mart, that he is leaving his baby momma soon as he off house arrest and we are getting an apartment!"

"How much longer he got?" Keyonnia asked while shaking dandruff from her ripped and faded black bike week shirt.

"I think like six months."

Phoenix was at her limit. She went to her room and got her headphones.

I can't have that dumb ass shit in my subconscious. Might wake up one day on some dumb shit like them.

Phoenix soon had the STD twins tuned out with neo soul music. Her mind drifted out the window over the kitchen sink. She remembered walking in the yard with her grandfather. He had a bad heart and would get winded quickly on their small walks. They would sit on the large grey toolbox in the far-left corner of the yard and talk. Her grandfather would sit and listen as Phoenix spoke about childhood nonsense. He hung onto every word which motivated her to keep speaking. The memory brought a smile to her face.

After an hour and a half of cleaning and scraping, Phoenix was finally finished. She'd been so involved with her chores, she hadn't realized the fake ass Pam and Gina had left the room. Relief washed over her. It wasn't until Phoenix started toward the fridge that she saw the black pile. They'd left a pile of hair and thread on the floor and table.

Rage filled her. Her ears became red hot. Tears fell from her eyes as she dropped to her knees. Grabbing the crystal necklace her grandfather gave her before he passed, Phoenix asked herself questions she had no answers to.

Why? What did I do to deserve this! Every day it's something. Cooking, cleaning, name-calling, stolen items. Why do they hate me so much?

The more she thought about growing up in her grandmother's house, the more tears fell. Phoenix never told anyone other than her grandfather that she remembered the night her mother was taken. Phoenix was around three or four at the time. The "flour" man came to the house like he did every other night. Phoenix could never really remember his face, but she did remember he was really nice to her. He always brought her gifts like toys or clothes. He smelled of cigars and aftershave.

"Time for little girls to go to bed so grown folks can talk business." Her mother smiled and kissed her on the forehead.

That was the last night Phoenix would see her mother without the presence of armed guards.

Boom! "Get down on the ground now!" ... "Check that room!" ... "Clear!" ... "Where is it?" ... "Get the kid!"

The house was filled with people in blue jackets and swat gear, with guns pointed in every direction. Phoenix saw her mother standing in the living room in a t-shirt and handcuffed, with pain and embarrassment written on her face.

"Mama! Mama!"

Tears ran down her mother's face.

A female officer took her away. "Mama...mama! I want my momma!"

Phoenix's pleas fell upon deaf ears. She was placed in the back of a cold dark police car.

Phoenix's daydream was broken by a woman's voice.

"Why are you crying?" Phoenix ignored her. "I

asked you a question... why are you crying? Crying ever fixed anything?"

The anger Phoenix felt came flooding back. This was her breaking point. Her grandmother had pushed her too far. Phoenix wiped the tears from her eyes. The old woman was about to get it. Phoenix jumped to her feet ready to release her anger.

She was shocked not to find the bitter woman in the kitchen, but a beautiful woman dressed to the nines. She wore a gold Michael Kors satin blouse half-buttoned, perfectly fitting black leather pants, red bottom heels, and what Phoenix thought had to be weave, down to her ass.

The woman propped a hand on her hip and flung her hair to one side. Phoenix noticed a wolf tattoo behind her left ear.

"From the look on your face...I'm not who you thought, hmm?"

Phoenix just glared.

"Speak girl! Cat got your damn tongue?"

Phoenix managed to blurt out a confused "No." She rapidly blinked her eyes and looked around the room.

Did some crazy-ass woman just break into this house?

Phoenix bit the inside of her cheek.

How in the hell...when in the hell did she get in? I thought I locked the screen door.

The woman began to walk a circle around Phoenix. Phoenix canvassed the room for what she might use as a weapon just in case this chick tried something. She eyed the knife in the dish rack.

The stranger sucked her teeth. "Boy... you real homely...we got to fix that."

Phoenix paused, rolled her neck and cocked her head to the side. The insult made Phoenix speak up. "Who are you and how did you get in here?"

The women rubbed her hands together. "I'm something like a fairy godmother, but way better baby!"

Phoenix smirked. "Let's get real. I'm grown and this ain't no fairy tale!" Phoenix eyed the stranger's neck tattoo again as she backed her way to the dish rack. The stranger peeped Phoenix's move.

"Before you pick up that knife, you may want to hear what I have to say."

"Look lady I don't know your Cookie Lyon looking ass! You popped up in my kitchen like you supposed to be here, and saying a whole lot of nothing!"

The stranger smiled. "Got a mouth like your mama."

Phoenix walked closer to the woman with her arms folded. "What the fuck you say?"

The stranger smiled. "Slow down Firebird."

Phoenix froze, no one called her that but her grandfather. The rush of emotions made Phoenix feel dizzy. Was she losing her mind? She leaned against the kitchen chair. Sitting on the table was a tan bag with the words Christian Louboutin written on it. Phoenix gathered her composure. "What's that?" she asked.

The woman smirked. "What's does it look like?"

Petrified, Phoenix slowly opened the box, inside was a pair of Christian Louboutin black asteroids. They were just her size, an 8.

"I see from the look on your face, you know what those are, but understand those are more than just heels. When you put these on, what's on the inside of you, the true you, will come out. The rules are simple. No one else but you can wear them, and when an opportunity presents itself, you should step out on faith and take it."

Phoenix was still confused. "I don't understand any of this."

The woman walked over to her and looked Phoenix in the eye. "Let me put it this way... your tears of hurt and suffering have been heard. Faith is just stepping out and believing. Take the shoes and when an opportunity comes, take it...Do you want a better life?Well, here it is."

Phoenix hung onto those words for a moment. "Want a better life." Hell yeah, she wanted better. She thought she deserved better. Years of being treated like she wasn't shit was over. Taking baths in Keyonnia and Miesha's used water, watching Margaret sell her grandfather's belongings to strangers, and being spanked when she would cry for her mother. The worst of it all was Margaret allowing her younger brother to live with them, knowing he was a pedophile. He molested Phoenix for years after Wolf passed. When she finally had the courage to tell her grandmother, she was beaten severely and called a slut and a liar. She was only 11. The rapes didn't stop until she was 14 when Margaret found out her brother started molesting Miesha too. Then it was a big deal. She promptly had him arrested. Phoenix was done with the bullshit, anything had to be better than the life she was given.

Before Phoenix could speak the lady was gone.

"It's some crazy shit going on in here." Phoenix muttered.

The phone dinged. A new text came in.

You will work on the floor tonight as a host.

Phoenix's grandfather was in real estate and owned many properties in the area. Margaret had allowed her eldest brother to turn the two warehouses into cheap strip clubs. He only offered Phoenix two positions, either wait tables with no hourly wage; only tips, or strip.

"Perfect!" she said aloud. Things were looking up already. She could make some real money.The hosting job paid $7.75 an hour.

I will wear the shoes, but with what?

Miesha burst back into the kitchen. "Who the hell you in here talking to?"

Phoenix rolled her eyes and walked to the fridge. Empty.Not a scrap of food in it. "Did you really eat everything?"

Miesha sucked her teeth. "Oh, shit...those Those are red bottoms!" She pointed at the table. "How you get dem?!" She picked them up to get a closer look.

Phoenix snatched the box out of her cousin's hands. "Mind your business!"

"Everything here is my business. This is my house!" Miesha shot back.

Phoenix glared. "I don't know who in the hell gave you that fucked up though, but this is my grandpa's house!"

Her grandfather created his own community on his 40-acre property. There were two townhomes, six duplexes, and in the middle, was his house. A beautiful split level 4 bedroom, 3.5 baths. Her grandfather had a big heart, he allowed single mothers and young women starting out to live there until they got on their feet. Two years prior to Phoenix coming to live with him, he welcomed Keyonnia and Miesha in after their mother overdosed on heroin in a crack house.

Miesha laughed. "Not since my gammy told the doctors not to fix his heart and he died."

Phoenix slammed the shoebox on the table and bucked up to Miesha. "What the hell you just say?" Phoenix's hands began to shake.

Another laugh. "You heard me. The doctor said he needed a new heart and my gammy said 'no'... he died." She stated flatly.

Phoenix's breathing became labored. The pain of the night he died came rushing back to her. Phoenix was 10 and snuck into the hospital to see him. Margaret had kept her away. Her grandfather lit up like a Christmas tree when he saw Phoenix.

"Hey Firebird, I'll be home soon." he kissed her on the cheek. Phoenix was on cloud nine for the rest of the day.

She went home as if she had been in school all day. Margaret met her at the door. "Your grandfather is dead." The words fell from her mouth like lead bullets to Phoenix's heart. Margaret began to beat Phoenix for every tear she dropped. Miesha and Keyonnia laughed.

The memory was the fuel to her fire. Phoenix's heart started to pound, her vision dimmed, her teeth clenched. She slapped Miesha before she even realized her hand was moving.

That was the match that lit the bomb. They slammed each other around the kitchen. The dish rack hit the floor and plates shattered with a loud crash. Miesha tried to claw at Phoenix's face.

Wham! Phoenix's right fist landed on Miesha's nose. Blinded by blood, Miesha charged at Phoenix and bit her left nipple.

"You stupid bitch!" Phoenix screamed in pain. Phoenix grabbed Miesha by her hair and slung her face-first into the fridge.

Keyonnia ran into the kitchen. "Granny!"

They started throwing each other around, slamming into cabinets and falling into the table. Her grandmother ran into the kitchen screaming. "What the hell is going' on?!"

Each girl landed one last punch before stopping.

Miesha spoke first. "Granny, she stole my shoes!"

Phoenix reeled. "Stop lying! Your fat ass feet can't wear those shoes!"

Keyonnia chimed in. "Granny Phoenix lying! Those are Miesha's red bottoms."

Phoenix couldn't believe it. "Those are too small for you!"

Margaret took the shoes. "Phoenix, you always been a liar. But now a thief too?" She shook her head like she wasn't too surprised.

"But...." was the only word Phoenix managed to say before her grandmother smacked her. "Get out my house before I call the police." The old woman yelled. She always wondered why her grandmother treated her so terribly and treated them like gold. She was Margaret's blood, not them.

Miesha and Keyonnia started to laugh. A second

later, Miesha pushed Phoenix out the door and slammed it in her face.

Phoenix's chest tightened as she slammed her fist against the ground. It was getting hard to breathe. She walked to the edge of the yard by her grandfather's old grey metal toolbox and dropped to her knees. The weight of the world was on her shoulders. And it was too heavy.

"There you go again with all that crying." a now-familiar female voice spoke.

"They took the shoes." Phoenix sobbed.

"And? Go get them!" The lady helped Phoenix to her feet, then continued. "You give up too easily. Learn to stand up for yourself."

A wave of confidence washed over Phoenix. She stood taller, her eyes narrowed and her chest stuck out. A second wave of energy followed. She turned and looked at the house. Walking back to the door, Phoenix kicked it in. The women inside stared in disbelief.

"Where are my shoes?" Phoenix demanded.

Keyonnia jumped up. Phoenix's stare was full of authority and warning, Bitch, don't try me!

Keyonnia's mouth dropped open. She was in shock. Flames of rage and anger were in Phoenix's eyes.

She ransacked the house in search for her shoes. Miesha sat at the table holding her broken nose. Keyonnia quickly disappeared. Margaret followed behind Phoenix nervously.Margaret pushed Phoenix and stood in the doorway of her room.

"Move or I will move you!" Phoenix said through clenched teeth.

Margaret braced herself. "Girls!" she screamed.

Keyonnia ran up and pushed Phoenix from behind, knocking her down.She banged Phoenix's head on the floor. "You're not getting those shoes!" She spit in Phoenix's face.

Phoenix kneed her in the stomach. Keyonnia rolled over in pain. She kicked Keyonnia between the legs, then quickly turned to Margaret and wrapped her fingers around her neck. Margaret tried to scratch Phoenix's eyes but missed. Phoenix squeezed until Margaret stopped moving. She dropped her almost breathless body letting her fall to the floor and walked toward the closet.

Phoenix found the shoes in Margaret's closet on top of a chest of drawers.

"Open the drawer." a voice whispered inside of her head. Phoenix felt compelled to listen to the voice. She slowly opened the top drawer. Inside were pictures of women and newspaper clippings. She moved them to the side. She found her grandfather's empty money clip and lighter. She closed that drawer and moved to the next. She checked over her shoulder and Margaret was still laid out on the floor. The second drawer was filled with paperwork. Some of the envelopes had DSS written on the outside of them. Phoenix did not recognize the names they were addressed to.She opened the last drawer.

Inside were several folders. Margaret began to moan as she started to regain consciousness. Phoenix rushed to open the folder to read what was inside. Her hands shook and her ears began to burn. It was like lightning striking as the realization of what she was reading came to her. She could feel butterflies in the pit of her stomach. This was her grandfather's last will and testament.

Margaret rushed to the closet door. "Get out of there!"

Phoenix slammed the closet door in Margaret's face and continued to read as Margaret banged on the door.He'd left Phoenix the houses. The land and his warehouse property was left to her mother.

Phoenix swung open the closet door with the will in hand. Her grandmother stood in the doorway, her chocolate skin lost color when she saw what Phoenix had found. Her mouth hung open, she was speechless...for once.Her lie was exposed. Phoenix brushed by her with her head held high, walking into the living room. All three women stood in awe of Phoenix. They had never seen this side of her. She stood tall, 6' 2 in her new six-inch red bottoms.

Phoenix didn't need Margaret, Margaret needed her! She pulled out her cell phone and looked at the time. She grinned.

"You bitches got five minutes to get the hell out of MY house! Margaret, no need to pack... I'll send you your shit!" she said, calling her by her first name to show total disrespect.

"Granny, what is she talking about?"

Keyonnia pleaded, she was panic-stricken. She searched Margaret's face for answers, but she saw there were none.

Out of desperation, Margaret reached for the paper. "What the hell are you talking about Phoenix? You getting to be real disrespectful!" Her voice quivered. Phoenix jerked it back.

"Phoenix give me that paper!"

Phoenix stepped back and pre-dialed 911. "Bitch don't play with me. You know damn well what this paper says! Get out or get thrown out!"

Margaret put her head down and mumbled. "Y'all get your stuff."

"I ain't going nowhere." Miesha ignored her grandmother. "Grandpa died, Granny gets everything."

Phoenix laughed. "Naw, this paper...this paper right here bitch... that Granny tried to hide says otherwise. But I know you a little slow, so I will help you. This is my house... y'all homeless... Get the fuck out!"

C H A P T E R   T W O

The Queen Has Landed

free after doing seventeen years was a lot to handle. She was nervous and a little scared, which was out of character for her. Even though she kept in touch with the outside world, living in it would still be a shock to her system.

Phoenix checked the master bedroom one last time. She wanted everything to be perfect. Her mom would need to get adjusted, and Phoenix wanted to help. She knew that Legacy had limited contact with the outside world. Her mother Margaret made sure of that, never allowing Phoenix to visit her after Wolf died. Margaret never even spoke of Legacy, it was as if she never existed.

She went into the money stash to refurbish the bedroom and the rest of the house. Her grandmother's presence in the house had been erased. Now Phoenix could move forward and start anew with her mother. As the limo got closer to the prison, Phoenix could feel the butterflies in her stomach. Even though she had been visiting her mother every weekend since she turned 18, this was different.

The limo pulled up to the women's prison. It looked cold and hard with bars on the windows and barb wire. Phoenix was blown away at the sight of her mother. At 40 years old, Legacy was at her prime. The seventeen years in prison had no effect on her appearance. In fact, it stopped time. She still had the body of a 25-year-old swimsuit model. The pink halter jumpsuit Phoenix bought her fit perfectly.

"Let me find out you rented a limo for me!" She exclaimed excitedly as she walked from the prison gates.

"Nothing but the best for the queen!" Their embrace was as tight as the last, Phoenix was 4 but she remembered watching her mom leave and the loving hug she gave her.

"Let's get a selfie right quick." Phoenix posted the pic on Instagram with the caption;

"The Queen has landed!"

* * *

"Freeze!" Legacy jumped from her sleep, heart racing. "Put your hands where we can see!"

"What the fuck?!" Legacy wiped the sleep from her eyes to see what was happening. The room was filled with FBI agents, and all guns were pointed at the bed. She slowly removed the covers to reveal her naked body. Her nightmare of guns and police became a reality. She looked to find her bed empty, he was gone. Her mind was racing as she tried to figure out what to do.

"Put your hands behind your head!"

"Y'all are such assholes... let her put some clothes on."

A female deputy brought Legacy a t-shirt to put on.

"Who is in the house with you?" the deputy asked.

"My daughter is in the other room, she is four." The deputy escorted Legacy and Phoenix downstairs to the living room.

"Calm down Phee, it's ok." Legacy tried to soothe her daughter's fears.

"Where's the stash?" an officer inquired. Legacy stared stone-faced at the officer as they began to ransack the house.

"Bingo... Got em."

The officer brought 10 bricks of cocaine and weed into the living room and dropped them on the floor. Another officer brought guns and money.

"Little girl, tell your momma bye because you won't be seeing her for a while." the officer beamed from his finding. Legacy spit at his feet.

* * *

Margaret was frying bologna when her phone rang.

"Hello." She answered.

"She's out." The voice on the other end replied dryly.

"Who is this?"

"She's on the way to the house." The voice said, ignoring her question.

"Karen?"

"Yes... now, what are you going to do? I am not going down for that shit Red!"

Margaret was taken aback at her nickname. No one had called her Red in years.

"I'll handle it."

"You better." And with that, Karen ended the call.

"Fuck!" Margaret yelled as she slung her cup across the room. It shattered against the wall, leaving a long trail of brown coffee. Keyonnia jumped from the couch.

"What the fuck wrong with you?" Margaret was silent. "Shit I'm trying to sleep before I go out tonight," Keyonnia complained.

Margaret glared at her. The one-room motel room was not big enough for the both of them, and Keyonnia was wearing out her welcome. They lucked up on the place because Miesha made a deal with the owner to work as a maid in exchange for two rooms, so of course, Miesha kept a room to herself. Margaret had to come up with a plan quick. She was in no position at the moment to handle the wrath that was coming her way. Only a fool would think there was no payback. Hell, she thought, Legacy had seventeen years to think of a plan. Margaret had to think and she had to do it quickly, she turned off the hot plate, leaving her bologna, and walked outside.   ***

As Phoenix and Legacy pulled up to the house, Phoenix notices a somber look come across her mother's face.

"What's the wrong Ma?"

"Things have changed a lot." Legacy's heart dropped as the limo pulled up to the desolate property. Wolf had the place booming back in the day. No team came close to what he had. Every duplex was filled with bad bitches, and each crib was laid out with the finest furnishings. Now it was a ghost town. Empty boarded up duplexes, and unkempt lawns. She was back home now. Her mother's dark cloud would soon be wiped out, and Wolf's dream would live on. Legacy was an unstoppable force. Her mind was made up. Death would fall upon anyone who got in her way, including Margaret, mother or not. Legacy made a mental note to make sure she got the property back to its prime. She would use the money from the stash spot to get things fixed. She looked around and knew it would be hard work.

They walked into the house. Legacy took in a deep breath and released it slowly.

"Ok, we have seven hours before your welcome home party tonight at the club."

"Thank God! I need to sit my ass in some water!" her mother said jokingly, yet serious at the same time.

Phoenix laughed at the realness her mother was giving her.

"You have no idea what it's like not being able to take a bath and all that damn hair! Them bitches shed like hell! Your skin will crawl when you get relaxed and look on the wall and see a curly black pubic hair!" Legacy cringed at the memory.

"Well Ma, your home now!"

Phoenix walked her to the master bedroom. Emotion swept over Legacy. The thought of a real bed and a hot bath. Phoenix gave her mother a hug.

"I missed you."

Legacy fought her emotions, trying not to seem soft in front of her daughter.

"Give me a few to get my mind around being home."

"Ok... I'll check on you in a few." Phoenix said as she left the room.

* * *

Legacy dreaded getting a new bunkmate.

I hope this bitch knows what's up...

To her surprise, the lady was much older. Legacy thought this might be in her favor, as older ladies usually stayed to themselves. The younger ones always tried you. Legacy pretended to read as the woman got settled.

"You looked like your mother." The woman smiled.

"Excuse me?" Legacy could feel her attitude crawled up the back of her neck.

"That Seminole Indian is all over you. You are beautiful just like Sultana."

"Sorry, you got me mixed up with someone else. My Mama's name is Margaret." Legacy spat back.

"No, I know who you are Legacy."

The older woman sat down on the bottom bunk. She had Legacy's attention. She jumped down from the top bunk and sat at the table in their small cell.

"How do you know me?"

The older smiled. "I know more than people think I do."

She pulled a little black book from her pants. "This book has saved my life with what it knows." She handed the book to Legacy. On the worn cover was Wolf's name.

"I knew your father and your real mother."

* * *

Legacy took in the sight of her own private bathroom. The floral scented candles were perfect. She started the hot water and steam quickly began to cover the mirror. Legacy wiped the mirror and stared at herself. For seventeen years she had to look at her reflection in shiny metal. Looking into a real mirror was so different. She could see all her features clearly now.

Once the water started getting cold, Legacy lathered her body and rinsed one last time before stepping out. She felt the weight of the world on her shoulders. Her life was on pause while in prison. Today, the play button was finally pressed. She took her time drying off. Privacy was a strange experience. No one was watching or rushing her. It felt good not to have to watch her back. She opened the double door that lead from her master bath to her master bedroom. Phoenix had it decked out in the finest linens. The sheets on her king-sized bed were snow-white satin, and a down feather comforter topped it off.

Legacy dropped her towel and laid across the bed naked. She closed her eyes and for the first time in seventeen years, she let go and let her mind drift.

* * *

"What do you mean?" Legacy's skin became flushed. She hated when people played with her mind. "My dad was a damn trick, and what do you mean real mother?" she said, clearly irritated.

"Legacy if you ain't ready for the truth tell me, you can save the attitude." The woman said calmly.

"Look you just came into my cell dropping shit. I don't know you from a can of paint!"

The woman turned and behind her right ear was Wolf's trademark tattoo that all his ladies had. The size and location gave rank. Right ear, Legacy knew this lady was somebody important.

"Now you ready to listen?" Legacy sat back in the chair, still holding on to the little black book, the woman had her full attention.

* * *

Legacy rolled over and looked at the time. She had four hours to get ready.

"Ma?" Phoenix call through the door. "You good?"

"Yeah, I fell asleep. I'm getting ready now."

"I was about to get something to eat, what you want?"

"Mmm, Chinese... shrimp fried rice."

Chinese and Italian were Legacy's favorite foods, and she couldn't wait to taste them again.

Legacy started to rub red velvet shea butter lotion on her body when the black book on the dresser caught her eye.

* * *

"I know what I'm about to tell you is a lot, but we don't have much time."

"Time for what?" Legacy asked.

"Wolf... your real father knew he was about to be stabbed in the back."

"Wait... wait! What!?"

"Wolf was your real father. Your mother was the one woman he actually let off. He had a lot of women in his stable, but he said only one was worth his seed."

Legacy's heart began to race and the information was smacking her in the face.

"Red.... Margaret was a jealous bitch! Once she found out that Sultana, your mother, was pregnant all hell broke loose. Sultana was everything Red wasn't. She was a full-blooded Seminole Indian. She had Wolf's nose wide open. She was loyal to him, something Red's evil ass could never be."

Legacy could feel her ears burn as blood rushed to them. She felt her hands start to shake.

"Red was on heroin... we called it chasin' dog back then. She was pregnant around the same time Sultana was, and lost the baby but didn't tell Wolf. She liked the attention he gave her. He felt bad that she was raped in prison and got pregnant. Red used that guilt against him."

"So where do I come in... I was..." Legacy interrupted.

"Let me finish... Red's cold-hearted ass cut you right out of Sultana, murdering her.... then she covered herself in her blood. She went to Wolf and acted like she'd just had you in the bathroom."

Tears ran down Legacy's face.

"She buried your mother in the back yard where she buried her real baby."

"Give me a minute... this is some heavy shit!" Legacy paced the floor.

"I'll give you tonight to take in what I just said."

* * *

"Ma... foods here." Phoenix announced happily.

Legacy pulled on a t-shirt and walked into the kitchen. She was startled to find Phoenix wasn't alone.

"My bad, I would have put clothes on if I knew your boyfriend was in here." Legacy said.

Phoenix looked at Tank.

"This is my homeboy, not my boyfriend." She said with a soft chuckle.

Tank had the look of a hungry man, his eyes drifted from her feet and landed on her breasts that were slightly showing through her shirt.

"Oh." Legacy smiled.

"He was dropping some stuff off." Phoenix noticed the look too. Tank was frozen. He was mesmerized by the tall brown skin beauty standing half-naked in the kitchen. Legacy took her food and walked back to her room. Without thinking, Tank licked his lips as her back view revealed two juicy round cheeks.

"Really!" Phoenix punched him in the arm. Tank grabbed his dick.

"Shit! I'm human and your mama is killer!"

"Eww, I don't want to hear that!" she said, sounding disgusted.

Tank gave Phoenix a grin and left. She stood in the kitchen shaking her head.

* * *

"I called this meeting to discuss your behavior and your request to start working."

Legacy shifted in her seat and tossed her long hair.

"Ok."

The warden cleared his throat and gathered the papers on his desk. He loosened his tie. "The nature of your crime determines if approved, what jobs you are eligible for."

Legacy licked her full lips slowly. "Alright." She purred.

The wardens gaze dropped to her half-buttoned jumpsuit. Legacy made sure to be bare underneath. She slowly leaned forward pretending to tie her shoe. She knew her breasts would shift and expose her nipple. Her tan areola started to show and the warden lost focus.

"You were saying..." She said seductively.

Legacy knew she had him. The warden shifted in his seat. His hard on was starting to be too much to bear.

"Yes... as I was saying..." his thoughts trailed off again. He needed to see those brown breasts, he yearned to suck her nipple.

"Let me help you with your thoughts." Legacy began to unbutton her jumpsuit, exposing her light brown breasts. The warden bit his lip. "You were going to give me a job working here in the office for you." She said matter-of-factly.

Legacy stood and let her jumpsuit drop to the floor. Her waist-length hair rested on her firm round ass.

"Aah." The warden moaned.

Legacy walked around the desk to find a wet spot in the warden's pants.

"Ooh... such a waste." She said, pretending to sound disappointed.

She brushed her nipples across his lips. "So, do I have the job?"

"Yes." He said almost too quickly.

He moaned as he filled his mouth with her full sweet breast. He slowly bent her over the desk and spread her ass cheeks. He slid his tongue into each hole slowly. Legacy moaned too. She threw her head back and came on his face, leaving a nice creamy film. A picture frame on his desk caught her eye. She turned to the warden.

"Who is that?" she asked, although she already knew him very well.

"He owns the prison."

"I thought this was a state prison?" She asked, attempting not to seem shocked.

"No, it's privately owned and controlled by the state."

"What's his name?" she asked.

"Jefferson."

A chill ran up her spine. She slipped back into her jumpsuit.

"Same time tomorrow?" The warden asked with a grin. Legacy winked at him as she was led back to her cell.

* * *

Legacy stepped out of the bedroom ready to change history. Phoenix raced to the coffee table to get her phone.

"Hold on Ma, let me get my phone. You shittin' on em' hard!"

Legacy tossed back her natural waist-length brown hair and blushed. She looked Phoenix straight in the eye. "This is the night that will change everything. I need you to trust me and follow my lead."

Phoenix was a little confused but shook her head in agreement.

"After tonight, you will go from working at the club to owning it." She said proudly.

"How?"

Legacy dropped the black book on the table. "With this and the packaging envelope, I mailed here some time ago."

Confusion was written all over Phoenix's face.

"To put it simply, men will do ANYTHING for pussy... and I have the slip to prove it. They owe Wolf and I'm cashing in. I need you to back me. My mother was sloppy and kept a trail. In this book is everybody, from doctors, lawyers and your father."

"Ma... what is going on? And you ain't never talked about my daddy." Phoenix was truly puzzled.

"It's too much to say tonight, but trust! Shit is about to get real."

When they pulled up to the club, Legacy looked over at her daughter. "You got my back baby girl?"

Phoenix looked deep into her mother's eyes. "1000!"

CHAPTER THREE

King

Boom...Boom...Boom.

Diamond jumped up in her king-sized bed startled, and still half asleep.

Boom...Boom...Boom.

Knocking pillows to the floor she yelled. "Who the hell knocking like the damn police?!"

Boom...Boom.

"Coming!" she yelled down the empty hallway. Diamond threw on her boyfriend's t-shirt. The smell of his Egyptian musk was still on it. She inhaled deeply, taking in his scent, then grabbed her 9mm from her nightstand and stomped down the hall.

"Who is it?!"

Click Click.

Diamond cocked her gun. She hoped whoever was on the other side heard the attitude in her words and the cocking of her pistol.

Can't even get some damn sleep....

"Girl!" A female voice yelled back. "It's me! Open the door."

"Who the fuck is me?!" Diamond stood on her tiptoes and looked through the peephole. "Phee!" Diamond let a breath of relief. It was her bestie, Phoenix. The two met on the playground when they were little girls. They had grown close to each other as Diamond was always taking up for Phoenix. They grew to be closer than friends, they were sisters. Even though there were only six months between them, Diamond acted like the big sister.

"Girl! You 'bout to get shot knocking on the door like that!" Diamond opened the door as she rubbed the cold from her eyes.

Phoenix didn't waste time, she quickly brushed past Diamond into the apartment. "You home alone?"

"Yea, Quian went out of town on a run. What's up?"

"Check yo' page." Phoenix insisted.

"Bitch, you woke me up over Facebook?"

"Trust...look at your page" Phoenix walked past her and sat on the couch with her legs crossed.

Diamond placed her gun on the table then shuffled into the bedroom to get her phone. She rolled her eyes as she logged in.

"Keep rolling your eyes and they gone get stuck like that!" Phoenix joked.

"This better be good." Diamond smirked.

"Trust!" Phoenix sat back on the couch. Diamond sat next to her with her legs crossed. It took a few seconds for the page images to load. Phoenix braced herself for Diamond's reaction.

"I swear this Wi-Fi is some bull.... What the fuck!" Diamond yelled.

The first image on her wall was of an ashy light skin female face down, ass up with Quian, her supposed to be nigga. He was balls deep in the bitch's pussy posing for a selfie. Diamond stared at the picture, her mouth dropped open, and for a moment she stopped breathing. She frantically searched her mind for a reason to say it wasn't him. She found none. It was without a doubt him. The tattoo on his neck was a dead giveaway. It was his mother's name, Sophia. Diamond stood to her feet with her mouth gaping open. The next picture was of the chick's hairy tarantula like legs wrapped around his back, his winged tattoo was glaring at her. Diamond's ears started to heat up as she saw the ratchet hand of this whore in his black wavy hair.

Phoenix took a deep breath. "There's more." With each scroll, the photos became more graphic.

Diamond gritted her teeth. "This muthafucka aint wear no rubber!" Tears welled in her eyes. It was like looking at a train wreck. Diamond couldn't turn away. "This bitch is a hot ass mess. Her lace front looks one of those fake blonde Halloween wigs from the dollar store!"

One picture came with a caption:

"You mad or nah! LOL! Yea bitch that's your man eating my ass in your bed, yea bitch that's your man hittin' me from the back raw as I wear yo heels, LOL, hug and kisses bitch!"

Diamond's flesh crawled. He was putting his pretty pink lips on that nasty rusty neck...lips he had just had on her. Diamond stood and walked robotic like to the bedroom and stood in the doorway. Her mind drifted to the night before. He walked in with his manly swagger. From the look on his face, she knew he was up to something.

"I got to go make a run for ya pops so I won't be home." His voice was smooth as silk.

Diamond shifted in the bed. "How long you gon' be gone?"

He licked his lips. "Two days max. You know how I drive." He shot Diamond a look. He walked closer to the bed and cocked his red ball cap to the right. "Let me give you a reason to be a good girl." He gave another million-dollar smile. He slowly pulled back the sheets. The soft touch of his long beard hair sent shockwaves through her body. The mere thought of that dope boy dick drove her crazy.

Thoughts of their love making began to mix with the current images of him and that basic bitch. Diamond bit her lip. The bed sheets in the picture were the sheets she was just sleeping in. That bastard didn't even have the decency to change the sheets. She walked to the bed and snatched the sheets off. She stood the mattress on its side and pushed it against the wall.

"Aghhh!" She yelled as she knocked his cologne bottles to the floor. A few of them shattered and broke. The mixture of the different scents filled the room.

Phoenix wrapped her arms around Diamond to stop her from shaking. "So, what we gone do?"

Diamond's ears burned, her heart was going to beat out of her chest, and her head swam. Phoenix guided Diamond back in the living room to sit on the couch. "Diamond sit down and breathe... I know this hurts, and I'm sorry. Whatever you want to do you know I got you."

Diamond searched her mind for some kind of sign. This made no sense. The nigga had it good. He woke up to head in bed every morning and the pussy stayed wet. Hell, Diamond plugged him to her father and his connect, so he was eatin' good. He was hurting for nothing, he had it good all the way around. It made no sense to her, there was no reason other than being a nigga. Fucking what he could because the stupid bitch let him. Now they both had to pay. The bitch could have walked, but posting on Facebook was too bold and Diamond wasn't going out like that. Diamond replied to the post with one word...

Noted.

* * *

Miller leaned in, nose to nose with Doc. His office suddenly felt smaller. Doc shifted his weight from one leg to the other nervously. The stranger leaning in the corner made him even more uncomfortable. He was one creepy looking dude, and he never said a word to anyone. Just always there with Miller, watching in the shadows.

"Look me in eyes so I know we got an understanding." Miller's eyes bore a hole into Doc.

Doc took a deep breath. "What's up?"

"Now when you take this pack, you signing yo' soul to me! I want my money, so don't fuck with me. We cool, but this is business." Miller adjusted his collar.

Doc backed up a few steps. "Ay man, no need to get so deep. I got dis. I been gettin' money."

"I'm talking as deep as it gets! You take this pack, you signing your soul over. Understood?" Miller said looking him straight in the eyes. His face was deathly serious.

"Yeah, Miller, I understand." Doc said, ready to get his pack and roll. The whole scene was creeping him out.

Standing at the far-left of the room, Diamond laughed under her breath. Her father was always so dramatic when he made deals with the young hustlers. Telling niggas they signing their soul away for a little product. Then the dude Doc was a loser. No way she could respect a 30-year-old nigga gettin' work on consignment.

No boo, you not gettin' money.

Miller motioned for her. "Diamond, inventory this shit up." he barked.

Doc and Miller dapped up to seal the deal. The silent stranger, who'd been standing in the corner, left the room. He took the uneasy chill in the air with him. After twenty-five years together in the dope game, Miller could read his green-eyed business partner like a book. He wasn't pleased with this move with Doc.

While placing the last brick in the duffle bag, Doc grabbed Diamond's hand. "After dis come up...I can buy you."

Diamond threw her head back as she laughed. "Nigga please! After you fuck up this come up, you won't be breathing. You have no hustle or business about yo self. You not on my level." She strutted out of the office.

As Doc walked out of Millers office to his car, he mumbled, "Bitch!"

Diamond rolled her eyes and pulled out her cell phone. She called her uncle. "Yo Unk, you pick up the package?"

"Yea baby girl it's waiting on you at the club house." His calm voice came through the receiver loud and clear.

"Cool, I'll be there soon as I'm done with work". A small smile came across her face. It was time to show how hard diamonds can cut.

Diamond and Phoenix arrived at the clubhouse within an hour. "Unk where the pack?"

The oldest of Diamond's seven uncles lead her into the bedroom. Tied to the bed and stripped of his clothes was Quian.

Diamond turned to Phoenix. "I want to talk to him alone."

Phoenix nodded and walked into the kitchen. Diamond slowly walked into the dark room and turned on a lamp that sat on the dresser across from the foot of the bed. The shocked expression on Quian's face quickly turned to anger.

"What the fuck you doing? Untie me bitch!"

Diamond raised her left eyebrow. "Bitch!... Wow!"

Quian attempted to pull at the ropes.

"First you get bold and fuck a bitch in my house!" Diamond paced the floor.

"Man, what the fuck you talking about?"

Diamond pulled out her cell phone and shoved the images in Quian's face.

"Nigga don't play with me! The dumb bitch posted the shit on Facebook!" Diamond could see on his face he didn't know they were posted. She picked up a tube of BenGay ointment from the dresser. "I see you like when a bitch jack yo dick." Diamond smiled.

"Come on Diamond, stop playing." His voice went up an octave.

"Who said this was a game?!" Diamond shot daggers with her eyes. She squeezed a handful of cream into her hand and slowly walked to the bed. Quian frantically tugged at the strong ropes, making the bed shake.

"Diamond for real... stop. This shit ain't funny!" he begged.

"Good, because the shit posted to my wall ain't either!"

"I didn't know she was going to do it!"

Diamond slow stroked his dick and balls, coating them in BenGay. She smiled as his dick got hard. She put a large glob in the tip and stepped away from the bed.

"Really nigga! That's all you can say? That's some deep shit, you know that."

"FUUUUCK!" He screamed as the cream began to heat up, setting his balls on fire. "Fuck man! It was just some pussy!" He pleaded. Beads of sweat popped from his forehead.

"Fuck you nigga... in my bed! Raw! You don't know who she fuckin' or what she got!"

Quian looked away as he spoke the next words. "Man, I know because I been with her long as I been wit you..." Quian knew he had fucked up.

Diamond started to laugh. He sealed his fate.

He was a liar from day one. It was another slap in Diamond's face. Quian tried to hide his fear as the heat of the ointment drastically increased to an unbearable level. His dick was on fire.

"So, you were cheating the whole time? That bitch ain't even on my level nigga. I put you on. Yo pockets stayed fat because of me!"

Foam started to collect in the corners of his mouth. "Fuck you bitch!" Quian shouted in pain as tears ran down his face.

"Naw nigga, fuck you!" Diamond walked out the room. She looked at her uncle. "Handle that!"

"Diiiiamond!" Quian's helpless screams fell on deaf ears. He no longer mattered to Diamond. He was dead to her.

* * *

Three weeks later, Miller met his business partner Lee, at Albert's "The Den" strip club. Lee, as he was known on the streets, was a 'no radio playin' type from New Orleans. He was all business. Miller was about the money, and Lee was about making folks bow down to the dollar. Since partnering up with Lee, Miller expanded his territory and made more money than he could spend.

They took a private VIP room in the back. It was a decent sized room with low lighting. The booth's seating was leather with a gold trimmed glass coffee table and red velvet walls. Off to each side were gold stripper poles that only the elite, AKA, the baddest bitches could strip on. Lee reared back in his booth seat. He pulled out a Macanudo cigar and lit it with a wooden match. His piercing eyes bore a hole into Miller.

"You know Doc is not going to cut it." Lee hissed.

"Hold on." Miller shifted in his seat, uncomfortable. He ordered the strippers to leave the room. It felt as if the walls were closing in on him. "Dis deal was no good from the jump. Not worth the paper it's written on." He slowly exhaled a ring of smoke from his cigarette. "I need someone pure to sell dey soul for dat money!"

"Hell yea, he done fucked up the pack already... try to call him." Lee sipped his Hennessy. His voice was deep and rumbled in his chest when he spoke.

"Fuck." Miller pulled out his phone and punched the numbers. Deep down he knew Lee was right. Word on the street was Doc's was flashy and quick to sell to anyone. After one ring, Miller was sent straight to voicemail. Miller took a big swig his Rosé and swallowed hard. He was in debt because of Doc's fumble. He needed someone new, and quick.

* * *

"Shit!" King hit the ground hard after hopping over the fence. The rain made it hard for him to see. He scraped his leg and could feel the warm blood run into his sock. He didn't have time to stop. The undercover was hot on his heels.

He'd tried to tell Doc something wasn't right. King never made a deal when his gut told him not to. His mom always told him, "Not all money is good money." The last time King looked back, he'd seen Doc being tackled to the muddy ground. King was trying not to panic. That would only get him caught. He had to think smart. He was running out of breath, and his legs wanted to give out. He had to shake the cop and quick. King knew the creek could slow the undercover down, and he could lose the cop in the swamp. He zigged and zagged his way to the creek. The moss on the rocks under his feet made it like running on ice.

From the muffled sounds, King knew the cop was hiding in the underbrush. He tried to pace his breathing so it couldn't be heard. King knew he had outgrown these groups of niggas. They were small minded and sloppy. He checked the time on his phone. It had been an hour since he last heard anything move in the swamp. He'd made it. The cops had given up, or were searching elsewhere.

King slowly crawled out of the brush. "Fuck man!" He looked down at his Jll's and they were destroyed. Covered in mud, sticks with briars, and God knows what else. King slowly limped home. Thank God, his mom was still at work. He wasn't in the mood to hear her mouth. Once that big red woman got started, it took her days to drop the subject.

* * *

Diamond couldn't believe she'd let Phoenix talk her into going out for a sip. Diamond hadn't been out since Daquian went missing. Him and that bitch. She laughed a little at the word "missing." The two were dressed to the nines. Diamond was wearing a long sleeved, form fitting leather splicing black and white jumpsuit. Her waist length hair was twisted in honey blonde faux locs. Phoenix was wearing a floral print bodycon jumpsuit, and her hair was twisted in a bun. They never let anyone see them off their game.

"Let's get a drink!" Phoenix yelled over the music. They ordered two Summer Rains, a fruity but strong drink.

"It's too loud... Let's go outside!" Diamond and Phoenix made their way outside. As they did, Diamond's Christian Louboutin Daffodil heel went into a small hole that sent her headed to the ground face first.

"Gotcha shawty."

Diamond found herself face to face with a nice chocolate brown. His head and face was clean shaven, all but the jet-black hair on his chin. He was wearing Gucci shades and purp for cologne. Diamond briefly lost herself when she looked at his full thick lips. His large hands gently supported her back.

"Thanks." Diamond bit her lips before more words escaped. He flashed her a pearly white smile. Diamond felt herself mesmerized. She had to work to bring herself back.

"Since I saved yo' life and everything, you owe me yo' number." His tongue glided across his lips as he licked them. Damn Diamond thought.

"Oh really!? How about you give me yours, and I call you."

"That's what's up." He flashed another grin and stroked his beard. Diamond felt her honeypot jump.

"What's your name?"

"King." He continued to stroke the hair on his chin as he spoke.

Diamond saved his number and walked away. She could feel his eyes on her ass. Her jumpsuit was fitting, and no panties meant her ass was jiggling like a bowl of Jell-O.

"My nigga you know who that is?" King turned to his home boy Tank, who interrupted him watching Diamond slowly walk away.

"What's up?" They dap up. "Naw man...who that?"

Tank took a step back. "That's the trap princess Diamond, Miller's daughter, and the "7" are her uncles."

The 7 were known hired men. For the right price, they could make anything and anyone disappear without a trace.

King looked at his Honda accord. Tanked tapped him on the shoulder. "Yea nigga, you want that you gotta step it up. She royalty my nigga!"

King stood in amazement as he watched Diamond start her white BMW M4. He wasn't sure what it was about her, but he had to have her. And for the first time, he wasn't speaking on fuckin'. He wanted to get to know her...then fuck. His day dream was rudely interrupted by the smell of cheap Avon perfume and a foreign hand on his crotch. His eyes trailed from the caramel hand with poorly polished nails until he found the source... a wide mouthed chick.

"Mmm, I got a taste for dat." Her gaze went to straight to his dick.

"What's up Kiki?"

"You!" she gave a devilish grin.

"Not right now." King brushed her hand off.

"Whaat?" Keyonnia exclaimed while sucking her teeth. "Don't nobody turn down my blazin' head!"

King hated the sound of her whiny voice. He looked her dead in the eyes "I just did." Pushing her to the side, King walked away. Keyonnia popped her gum, flicked her cheap imitation Brazilian weave and stormed off.

King contemplated Tank's words. He knew he couldn't get a chick like Diamond on no weed money. He had to step his game up, cocaine would do it. King rode by the trap spot. He waited outside to peep the scene, unsure if it was hot or not. He pulled a peach zigzag from his pocket. With his teeth, he tore open the wrapper. He licked the cigar to make it a little wet, then began to break up the purp and sprinkle it inside the moist cigar wrap.

Buzz Buzz.

King felt his cell go off in his pocket. He pulled it out and pressed the speaker button, placing the phone on the armrest as he finished rolling his blunt.

"Who dis?"

"Who the fuck you thank it is nigga? Yo baby mama!" the voice shrilled on the other end.

King paused, rolled his eyes, and took a deep breath. "What's up!?"

"Yo daughter need $200." The sassy woman on the other in spat out.

King grimaced. "Fo' what? she 3!"

"What you mean fo' what?" Keshia popped back with attitude.

Beep Beep

An incoming call cut off some of her words.

"Hold on...hold on...dats my mom's beepin' in." King clicked over before Keshia could object.

"Hello?"

"Boy...you need to get your shit together. I can't keep doin' this!"

"Woah, what you talking about Ma?" he asked.

"Dashia left yo 2-year-old son on the damn steps. I was on my way to the store and found him! You need to make better decisions...yo baby mommas ain't shit!"

"Aight, I'll be there in a sec." Click. He purposely hung up on his baby's mom Keshia too. King felt backed into a corner. He needed to do this...he had to do this.

Once he realized it was clear, King got out of the car. As he walked toward the door his heart began to race and his hands became sweaty. King didn't know what to expect. It had been two weeks since Doc was arrested and King didn't know if the house was hot or not. He pulled out a pack of Newport's. Even though he and Doc were homeboys, folks were known to change when they got under those hot lights. King lit his Newport as he walked through the house. He needed to get the work back to Miller. Once inside the house King saw the couch cushions were overturned, rugs were tossed to the corner, and the fridge was wide open. King dashed to his room. The padlock was still on the door. He quickly grabbed his pistol and the stash of cash. Doc's door was opened. The mattress had been flipped over. Whoever it was wasn't the brightest, the duffel bag was still in the top of the closet with work in it.

He arranged a meeting with Miller at The Den nightspot. King felt as if his stomach was trying to tell him something. His mouth became dry and his heart raced again. Doc had fucked up half the product. King knew the number one rule to the game was not to get high on your own supply. Doc fucked up because he wasn't about his business.

While Doc was MIA, King had to step up and double dip to keep their business going. Doc handled the cocaine, while he hustled the weed. His hands began to shake as he parked. He pressed play on his cd player. He needed to get in the zone. First there was a burst of base then Kevin Gates came through the speaker.

"I got 2 phones... 1 for the bitches, 1 for the plug..." That was the hype he needed. He placed his glock in his pants, just in case. King knew fuckin' wit a nigga's money was fuckin' wit yo life and the life of ya family. King couldn't handle the thought of his moms or kids getting hurt, especially behind some bull shit.

The bouncer directed King to the private office in the back. As King swaggered in, out the corner of his eye he saw Diamond at the bar. She flashed a flirty smile while sipping her drink. He gave her a wink back and stroked his beard as they locked eyes. Her ass was sittin' right in that white Michael Kors sundress. Her red bottoms had her calves poppin'. Yea, he had to make her his girl. His plan was to see her after the meeting. After tonight he would be the man and she would be by his side... his trap queen.

He walked into the office full of confidence after seeing her.

"Have a seat." Miller motioned for King to sit. He smiled showing his all gold teeth. "It's cool... you can relax..." Miller leaned in.

"King man, I been had my eye on you. I see what you been doin' wit dat weed man...and I like it!"

King looked confused.

"That little crew you and Doc got been makin' numbers, but I feel you can do more!"

King placed the duffel bag on the table. "Cool, but first I want to handle old business. This is what's left of what Doc had. The police took his money so I'm payin' his tab."

Miller looked at the two stacks of money on the table. From the shadows emerged his partner. He blew out a thick cloud of cigar smoke. He stood motionless for a while then briefly sat down beside Miller. Before leaving the room, the man whispered in Miller's ear.

Miller slowly opened the bag. It was stacked to the top. King tried to hold his shock. He knew the bag was half empty before he walked in.

"That deal was between me and Doc and I'll settle wit' him once he is out. This deal between me and you, understood? I see mad potential in you. Let's make dis money together."

Miller extended his hand to King.

"What's the ticket?" King asked.

"This deal is on face." Miller replied.

King felt uneasy, his gut was trying to tell him something, but he needed this deal to reach the next level. King paused for a moment. He knew if he chose this route he could end up dead or in jail. If he was killed his kids would grow up without a father. Who would protect his mother against her bad choices in men? If he went to prison then that would be a huge burden on his mother. His baby mommas weren't shit, they wouldn't put money on his books.

They all needed him. He couldn't have his mom depending on another nigga, he would be damned if another nigga took care of his kids. King also knew he had an expensive habit. His clothes had to be the best. A McDonald's job couldn't pay for his shoe habit. Fuck it!

King looked Miller in the eye. "I'm in." He dapped Miller sealing the deal.

He left the room feeling like the man. His next mission was Diamond. To his disappointment, she was gone. With the amount of work he had, he wanted to get it off him ASAP. He put the bag in the trunk of his car and got in the driver's seat. There was a knock on his window. It was Keyonnia again. He rolled down his window.

"What's up..."

Before he could finish his words, she slid half her body through the window. She unzipped his pants and went to work. King reclined his seat back. She felt too good for him to stop her. Keyonnia had all nine inches and his balls in her mouth. King threw his head back in pleasure. He felt the tip of his magic stick rub the back of her throat.

Buzz Buzz

"Hello?"

"Hey...This is Diamond."

"What's up, miss lady?"

Keyonnia ran her tongue around the tip as she bobbed her head. King was amazed. It was as if she had no bones in her neck.

"You... are you busy?"

"Nuttin'." he said as he released his load down Keyonnia's throat.

"Cause if you busy I understand."

"Naw, just in the car chillin', bout to pull out." He slid his dick out of her mouth. She licked the cum off the tip. He pushed her head out the window and pulled off.

"Good." Diamond purred. "Cause I wanted to know if you wanted to go out?"

"Let me make a drop, and I'm all yours."

* * *

Diamond hung up the phone.

"Good...Now I want you to keep an eye on him. The only way you can do that is to stay under him. Do whatever you gotta do." Miller instructed her.

"I don't like to be used." She pushed past her father toward the door.

"Fuck dat, dis business. You was fuckin dat lame ass nigga for free. You can do this for me."

Diamond shot daggers at him with her eyes. She was shocked her father was talking to her like that. Before she let him see her hurt, she tried to leave the room. Miller grabbed her arm.

"I don't have room for soft... tighten up." Diamond stared into his eyes. They were empty black pools. He had no soul left. She shook her head yes, that she understood. Diamond waited in the living room on the couch for King to call her back. She tried to wrap her brain around what was happening. One thing she did know for sure, the man she knew as her father was gone. With each dollar he made, a piece of him died. What she saw was just an empty shell. Tears welled in her eyes.

* * *

"Shit!" King had to adjust his pants so she couldn't see he had a hard on.

"What's up?"

Damn, he thought. She smelled like strawberries and cream. Tonight would be a struggle. He wanted to fuck the shit out of her right there in front of Miller's house.

"Do you like Hibachi?" he asked.

"Yes."

"Cool." He smiled.

That was the first date of many for King and Diamond. The product Miller gave him was the best on the streets. Nobody could beat him in price or quality. He had much more money than he knew what to do with.

He even started his own squad and re-upped every two weeks.

"Damn boy...you coming like clockwork." Miller met King with a smile and handshake.

"Shit... man... I don't know what's in dat shit, but they can't stop coming!"

"Shit, dats what's up." Miller started to load the bag. "While I got you here, I wanted to talk about you and Diamond."

"What's up?" King asked, looking Miller in the eyes.

"I see y'all getting close... I want you to know that has nothing to do with this here. I keep business and personal separate."

"I do too." They nodded at each other. King grabbed the pack and left. King was on a mission. Stack a million and get out the game.

CHAPTER FOUR

A King and His Diamond

Diamond lit four lavender scented candles around the tub as she ran herself a hot milk bath. She watched as the water and bubbles filled the large Jacuzzi tub. The porcelain oasis was her escape from the world. She placed a bottle of ice chilled Rosé and a wine glass by the side of the tub. She had been renting hotel suites for the past two months. Life was getting the best of her. Having the top floor suite to herself helped her relax.

First Quian and his ratchet side piece posted XXX pics of themselves on her Facebook wall, her daddy issues, and now she felt herself falling for one of her father's pawns. Diamond took a soft white towel and wiped the steam from the mirror. She studied her reflection then locked eyes with herself. It had been three months since her father Miller told her to get close to King. While looking deep into her own soulful brown eyes she twisted her honey colored coils into four Nubian knots.

King was everything the past and present men in her life were not. Unlike her smothering and overbearing seven uncles, he gave her space.

Unlike her father, he gave her affection. Unlike her last nigga, to her knowledge, he wasn't runnin' game. Diamond felt herself dancing on a very fine line between work, pleasure, and destruction. She didn't know how much longer she could withhold sex. King was starting to cloud her judgment and she couldn't stop it. Deep down she wasn't sure if she wanted to.

Diamond dropped her Egyptian robe around her feet. She slowly ran her hands over her velvet smooth brown skin. This was a habit she always had, she was attracted to herself. This drove men crazy. She slid into her warm water paradise. She let out a deep breath. This was the release she was looking for. She let her head fall back on the bath pillow. Since she had 'broken up' with Quian, she sold their house together and moved in with her uncles. She would drop dead before she moved back in with her father and her fake ass, coked out, stripper step mother Lace. She was no older then her. Living with seven men was starting to weigh on her. She had no space of her own and they were not the cleanest either. She had been renting hotel suites to take breaks. Diamond closed her eyes and let herself go. She let the feel of the warm water against her skin and the smell of the lavender candles invade her senses. They took her to a place beyond her present state.

"Who the fuck is that bitch!" yelled Kitten.

To her boyfriend's surprise, Kitten and their daughter were home early from shopping. Miller was caught with his pants down. Miller had the young woman bent over the kitchen table as he power drilled her. Another woman lay ass naked, passed out on the on the table with her legs gaped open. Her loud moans of ecstasy and pleasure drowned out the sound of the two women walking into the house.

"The bitch he fuckin' cause you ain't doin' it right!" The woman pulled Miller on top of her. "Come on baby, show her how dis pussy make you feeeel!" The woman licked her lips and gyrated her hips onto Miller.

Kitten shoved Miller out of the way and quickly two-pieced the loud mouthed naked woman.

"Ma!" Diamond screamed. Kitten ignored her daughter's plea. "Miller are you for real?" Kitten pleaded, waiting for an answer. Miller put his head down and pulled his pants up.

"So now you can't speak mothafucka!" Kittens caramel complexion went flush red. She gritted her teeth and swung punching Miller square in the jaw. The other woman swung her long blonde weave, wiped the blood from her nose, and grabbed Miller's gold-plated pistol off the table.

* * *

Knock Knock

Diamond jumped.

Knock Knock

She'd fallen asleep and her water had grown ice cold. The person at the door scared the hell out of her.

Bam Bam

"Hold on!" she yelled. She tried to wrap herself in a towel that didn't quite make it around her full hips and rushed to the door. It could be one of two people, Phoenix or King, they were the only two that knew she was at the hotel. She looked through the keyhole. To her relief it was King. She quickly undid her hair and shook out her curls before opening the door. She licked and softly bit her lips a little to make sure they were pink and juicy.

"What's up? Are you ok?" King looked to be in a trance when she opened the door. Once King caught the sight of Diamond soapy wet in a towel, his whole expression changed.

"Damn, that's how you do!?" a smile crawled across his face. King stroked his beard.

"I was taking bath." Diamond tried her best to ignore the energy growing between them and the warmth between her legs.

"Mm, don't let me interrupt..." King moaned playfully.

"The water's cold I needed to get out." Diamond tried to avoid eye contact.

"Damn, I was hoping to help." King smiled. His eyes blazed.

"Thanks, but I'm good." she teased. Diamond let him into the suite. Like always he was smelling like good kush. "Let me put something on. You can have a seat." Diamond walked into the bedroom of the suite and put on a red satin robe. She went back to the sitting area and sat on the love seat across from King. She crossed and tucked her legs under her. This gave her an excuse to show off a little thigh to him. Her nipples kept King's attention as he spoke.

"I'm having issues at my spot. Shit comin' up missin'. Can I keep this bag here until tomorrow? I got another spot where I can hold it. Just don't want to make too many moves in one day with it. Ya feel me?" King stated matter of factly.

"Yeah that's cool. I'm keeping the room for a week." Diamond played with her hair to try and hide her attraction.

"Look man... I fucks wit you, and when I fuck wit somebody, I look out. Give me a week and I'll have you a spot." King stated.

"You don't have to do that." Diamond wasn't used to hand-outs.

"Naw I don't like you living wit dem niggas, uncles or not, and staying at a room is too much. No strings attached, we got a bond. I'll always look out for you. Trust dat." King gave a warm smile. He walked to where Diamond was sitting, leaned in and kissed her gently on the lips. "My word is my bond." He put his hand on his heart. King looked down at his phone. "I got to make a run... I'll be back." He stood to leave.

"Wait...here." Diamond gave him a room key. They looked into each other's eyes.

* * *

As King approached the door, an uneasy feeling came over him. He pulled his pistol from his boxers. King slowly walked in the spot to find Keyonnia on the couch sleeping and trash bags of clothes all over the living room.

"Hey!" King tapped her on the foot to wake her.

Keyonnia rolled over and smiled. "Hey baby." She sat up and stretched.

"What are you doing?" He was trying to keep his cool.

"My folks kicked me out and I have no place to stay."

"What dat got to do wit me? And how the hell did you get in?"

"I figured I could stay with you... I had a key from awhile back...Doc gave me a copy."

King took a step back. "Say what?"

"Don't be mad... we fooled around, but you're my boo."

"Bitch please. All you do is suck my dick, I would never stick my dick in that black hole you call yo pussy! I knew some shit was missin'. Get the fuck out!" King roared in anger.

"King!" she fell to her knees. King snatched her back up to standing on her feet.

"Don't ever play wit me bitch!" He threw her and her clothes on the porch and slammed the door.

"Fuck you King! You ain't shit no way!" Keyonnia screamed and paced the porch.

King quickly gathered all his work.

Dis stupid bitch gone get me caught...fuck!

His mind began to race. He had too much to lose behind a stupid trick that wasn't his. King quickly rushed to the door. Keyonnia was still screaming at the top of her lungs. King swung the door open and grabbed her by her arm.

"What da fuck is wrong wit you?!" King's heart was racing.

The last thing he needed was to have the cops called, he had major weight on him. He would get 50 years plus easy for what he had. Keyonnia dropped to her knees again.

"Give me what I want and I will leave." she pleaded.

King felt trapped. "Fuck!" King said through clenched teeth. He pulled her back into the house, pulled his 9- inch pole out and shoved it in her mouth.

"Here, dis what you want!?" His voice was full of anger.

Keyonnia had to work to make him hard. His rage was blocking him from enjoying her. Like a fat girl with chocolate cake, she went to work. After fifteen minutes of bobbing and licking, he stopped resisting and enjoyed as she deep throated him until she gagged. It was an hour before she was able to get and enjoy all the cream from his chocolate log.

* * *

The detectives brought Doc into the interrogation room for their second round of questioning since his arrest 3 months before.

"Look all I know is dat they call the nigga "the stranger". He don't say much of shit, but when he do talk, he talk funny... like backwards... Cajun or Spanish, something like dat. He bring in all da work."

The officer wrote word for word as Doc spoke. They had heard of the stranger, but no one ever gave any details about him. The heavier detective plopped down in a chair with donut crumbs in his mustache.

"Look we want to help you, but you gotta help us." A crumb fell from the corner of his mouth as he spoke.

Doc sucked his teeth. He was no snitch. The other cop whose shirt buttons looked like they were holding on for dear life, dropped two pictures on the table. The cop extended his fat finger. "Who is that?"

Doc was fighting the urge to look but curiosity got the best of him. Heat rose from his collar. He saw two pictures, one of King getting head from Keyonnia, and the other of King with Diamond at the sip house. Doc's mind began to race.

King set me up. He wanted me out the way.

Doc couldn't believe King had sold him out for some bitch. Doc had been dicking Keyonnia down on the regular, and he was about to make his move with Diamond. He could tell she wanted him, and bad. King was fuckin' around with his bitch.

"Dat's King... he partners with the stranger. King fronts me." Doc figured if King could take the fall he could get in good wit Miller. Diamond would see he was the man and finally get with him.

The detectives gave each other a knowing look. They thought they had struck gold.

* * *

Diamond placed fresh flowers on her mother's grave. She couldn't believe it had only been a year. She hardly got any sleep due to the nightmares.

"Miller are you for real? So now you can't speak mothafucka?!" her mother gritted her teeth and swung, punching Miller square in the jaw. The other woman wiped the blood from her nose. She quickly leaned over, grabbing Miller's gun from the edge of the table. Two shots and Kitten dropped to the floor. Diamond's frantic screams echoed throughout the house.

She knelt down and began to pull the weeds, trying to make her mother's grave as beautiful as possible.

"Momma, I love you." She said aloud as tears streamed down her face. Diamond felt a hand on her shoulder. She looked up and saw her uncles quietly standing behind her, some of them holding their hats against their chests.

"You ok baby girl?" the shortest uncle asked.

"It's hard... I miss her so much!" She said between sobs. She slowly got to her feet and wiped her face. The oldest of the seven stood beside her.

"You know dis ain't over!" Diamond spoke to her mother's grave. She turned to hide her face and spoke one word.

"Noted."

* * *

King took a detour to one of his home girl's apartments. He wasn't sure if he was being followed or not. He stretched out on her couch. "Mercedes fix me some Kool-Aid." King's phone vibrated in his pocket. "Yea?" He hated to talk business over the phone.

"Look man, let me know what you gonna do before I come over there. I hate riding wit dat shit."

Mercedes sashayed into the living room and plopped on the couch. "Who you talking to?" She was very nosy. King just looked at her and wrapped up his conversation.

"Look, put these two bags in yo pussy and ride wit me." King stated without asking.

"Damn King, when you gonna put dat dick in it?" Mercedes whined.

"Cut it." He spoke with a straight face. He didn't like rude chicks, but it was business for him. He slapped her on her ass. She laughed and pushed the baggies inside her as she was told.

* * *

Lace finally talked Miller into letting her make a pick up. She met the connect at the 24 hours self-car wash off the main highway. Lace slid into the parked vehicle.

"Since when you make pick-ups?" Lee was a little confused. He was used to Diamond and Tank making the pickup runs.

Lace stuck her tongue in Lee's ear.

"Do you think I'm pretty?" She whispered, changing the subject.

"Yes. But Miller...." He moaned.

"Don't worry about him, keep our business between us, and you'll be aight." She told him.

She slid her hand down his chest slowly. She played a little with his chest hair before venturing lower. His body craved her and she knew it. She palmed his shaft and slow stroked it.

"Do you want me?" Lace purred.

"God, YES!" He said with excitement, fighting back the urge to release in her hand.

She took the small bottle filled with white powder from his console and made a line from the base to the head of his dick. She sniffed the line then engulfed his penis.

"Damn!" He yelled out.

"How bad do you want me?" she teased.

"Damn baby...my dick so hard it hurts."

She sniffed the line, licked around the head then slid his rod down her throat.

"Damn Diamond..."

Lace stopped "What did you call me?"

"Suck my dick!"

"Naw nigga...you called me Diamond."

"Stop trippin' Lace!" He tried to pull her mouth back to his dick.

Lace pushed against his hold. "You want her?"

"The truth...hell yeah!" he admitted.

"What? She ain't better than me!" she said with an attitude.

"Shit have you seen her? Those fat pink lips she keeps glossed. Pretty long real wavy hair going down her back." Lee trailed off.

He started to bite his lip and stroke himself the more he described her.

"When she wears a tank top her nipples poke out. Dem tits more than a mouthful. Dat ass is fat and bounces when she walks." He began to stroke himself faster and harder. "Dat pussy sits fat when she wears leggings...Aaah!" He shot off and cum went everywhere.

"Really nigga!?" Lace was pissed.

"Lick it." He ordered.

"Fuck you and dat bitch!" Lace stormed away from the car.

* * *

Phoenix and Diamond met up at Panera Bread for their weekly meeting. Wolf, Phoenix's grandfather, put Miller in charge of ensuring his daughter Legacy was taken care of in prison. Legacy, Phoenix's mother, was sentenced to seventeen years in prison for trafficking a distribution of narcotics.

Diamond noticed Phoenix kept looking over her shoulder. "What's wrong with you?"

"I swear I keep seeing this lady."

"What lady?" Diamond asked.

"I don't know who she is, but she keeps poppin' up and giving me advice."

Diamond raised one eyebrow. "Is there anything you have to tell me?!"

"Girl bye... I don't get high." Phoenix shot back.

"Hell, I'm just checking... but on the real some strange shit has been happening." Diamond joked.

"I talked to the lawyer today. He said he may be able to get the appeal in a few months." Phoenix said as she sipped her tea.

"Dats what's up." Diamond said with a smile. She handed Phoenix a duffle bag. "Here's the money Pops said to put on her books.

"Did you tell him what I did to Margaret?" Phoenix questioned.

"Yea... He wants to have a sit down with you." Diamond stated as she took a bite of her turkey sandwich.

"About what?!" Phoenix was a little nervous.

"He has to tell you. I don't know, but it has to do with Wolf." Diamond brushed it off.

"Tell him I said ok...just call me when he ready." Phoenix took a bite of her salad and spit it out.

"What's wrong with you?" Diamond laughed.

"Dis shit ain't got no type of flavor. This chicken didn't pass by no spice rack!" The two women laughed. Phoenix wiped her mouth.

* * *

King pulled up to an old run down brown wood panel home. "Pull those bags out for me ma." He stated without looking at her.

"You do it." she spoke as she licked her lips

"Come on now. Stop playin', dis business... you can suck it later." King was annoyed.

Mercedes lit up like a Christmas tree. She slowly pulled both baggies from her fur purse. King gave her specific instructions. "Wipe them off. Walk in, and there's a guy standing to the side. Hand those to him and he will give you an envelope. Bring it back... don't speak to him."

"Ok." Mercedes said as she hopped out of the car.

Buzz Buzz

King's phone went off. It was a text from Diamond.

I had to meet Phoenix to take her mom some money. I put the bag in the room safe code 67- 42- 83.

King texted back.

Cool... got a surprise for you tonight. Meet me at my spot. I'm cooking dinner.

King texted her the address to put in google maps.

Diamond didn't know what to expect when she got to King's house. She walked in trying to play off sniffing the air. Nothing... Diamond smelled nothing. King saw the look on her face and started to laugh.

"Girl, I can't cook." King sang.

"Really!" Diamond tried to keep a straight face but started to laugh.

"I'm joking... I got us some pizza... I just wanted to chill wit you, but my nerves won't let me do it at the room knowing all dat stuff in there. I don't shit where I sleep."

"Sooo... what are we going to do?" Diamond asked.

King led her into the living room. He had made a picnic pallet in front of the t.v with two boxes of pizza. Diamond thought it was kind of cute. She was hoping he wasn't a cheesy nigga. So far so good, he was keeping it realistic. They both sat down on the blanket. Diamond felt comfortable around him. They began to talk.

"So, what's up... what time your girl getting back?" Diamond looked him straight in the eye.

"What girl?" King said with a playful grin.

"King don't play me... I know who you are. There's no way you stay in this house by yourself." Diamond smiled back.

It was a cute three bedroom, two bath house. The furniture looked brand new.

"Why not?" King questioned.

"It's clean, and it actually has matchin' shit in it." Diamond blurted out. They both laughed.

"It's not a trap house?!" Diamond was confused.

"Shit, I like nice shit" King's eyes got chinky.

He leaned in and kissed her. "Like your lips..." He kissed her again.

Diamond leaned back. She didn't know why she couldn't keep her cool around him. King could see Diamond was fighting her feelings. He wasn't fully sure if she was real or wearing a mask. Either way tonight he was fucking her. He had to tread lightly. Fucking the plugs daughter could be dangerous.

Diamond made up her mind. She would call his bluff. Fuck him now, and if he never calls again, no loss. If he stuck around...great. She stood and slipped off her maxi dress. When Diamond turned around King couldn't contain himself. Seeing her naked ass sparked a fire.

"Stop don't move." King ordered.

Diamond froze, confused as to what he was doing. King rose to his knees behind her and he cupped both of her butt cheeks and kissed them. He slowly spread them apart and licked down her crack. She moaned. He slid his hand up her back and bent her forward. He slid his hands to her thighs and spread them, exposing her pink fruit. He began to suck her juices. After her body started to shake that was his cue to go to the next level. King stood up and kissed her back.

"Don't move stay just like that." King's voice became raspy.

Diamond was bent over his couch. She saw his pants hit the floor. She had to see what he was about to give her. He whipped out a long, fat, dark chocolate 9-inch rod. He was rock hard too.

"Damn," she whispered.

It took her breath once he slid in. Without warning she creamed on him.

"Damn! Keep cummin' on dis dick!" he groaned.

She looked back at him. He looked deep into her eyes. He leaned in and kissed her. She closed her eyes and let go. She melted as he pumped, losing count of the number of times she came. No words were spoken. They left earth together on waves of pleasure.

Hours had passed. They lay cuddled up together on the pallet.

"Move in wit me." King whispered in her ear.

"Say what?" Diamond was shocked.

"I mean, why not?" King kissed her softly on her forehead.

Diamonds mind started to race as fears of what could happen came over her.

"Yes." she was shocked by her own words. King smiled, pulled her closer and closed his eyes.

The next morning Diamond lay on the picnic setup, still sound asleep. King had just gotten out of the shower and stood over her, watching her sleep. For the first time, he felt like giving his heart to someone. He was no fool though, he knew Miller had something to do with them hooking up.

Smash! King heard glass breaking.

"King!" Screamed a whiney voice outside. "King! Muthafucka I know you hear me!"

Smash!

King ran to his window. Keyonnia was throwing bricks at his Range Rover.

"Shit!" he exclaimed.

"What's wrong baby?" Diamond rolled over.

King wanted to detain the monster outside before Diamond saw her.

"Nothing... Don't you move... I will be right back."

He threw on a pair of ball shorts and ran outside to find Keyonnia screaming and naked.

"Nigga I know you not laid up wit a bitch!"

"What the hell are you doing?" he yelled, looking at his damaged vehicle.

Keyonnia charged at him. He stepped to the side and she landed against his car.

"Where are yo clothes?"

"Why? You know I'm sexy! You know you want

me!" She threw herself to the ground and spread her legs.

"Bitch... bye... get the fuck out of here."

"King, fuck me, King... I love you."

"Bitch get off the drugs."

Keyonnia started to pleasure herself in the middle of the yard. King snatched her off the ground. "Get the fuck on Kiki!"

She began to cry. Her tears stopped once she saw Diamond standing in the doorway with nothing on but King's t-shirt.

"Dat bitch?! Dat bitch?!" Keyonnia pointed at Diamond. A crowd started to form around the three. King was pissed. He had never fucked this crazy bitch, and she was about to fuck up his plans. Diamond stepped out of the doorway towards them.

"Yea bitch! Surprise! It's me... I live here. That's my nigga and this my bitch!" Diamond pulled out her .22.

Keyonnia slowly backed away. King was highly impressed.

* * *

Doc was ready for his meeting with the DA. He would take the plea. He sat down on the cold, hard metal chair. He watched as they started the tape recorder. Doc began to make his statement.

"I am doing this under the agreement dat I get only 10 years, and I get put in protective custody."

"That's the deal." The district attorney said.

"Aight. The head of everything is King. I was under him. He wants everyone to think it's Miller when it's really him. Miller ain't had no real shit poppin' in years, he retired. King runs the whole show now."

Doc's plan was to cover his ass with Miller and to get rid of his competition. With King out of the picture he could have Diamond and be the hoods number one nigga.

***

Miller called Diamond in for a meeting.

"Look baby girl... we just got word Doc rolled over."

"I knew that bitch ass nigga wasn't built for the storm." Diamond said.

Miller's face went cold. "King has to take the fall."

Diamond's heart sank. The color ran from her face.

"I know y'all do whatever, but dis business. You knew that from the jump. If you caught real feelings for this nigga, that's on you! You mix business with pleasure, you create fire." He looked into her eyes to see if they were on the same page. "Diamond... look at me. I need you to follow orders... we are family... do you understand?" Miller pleaded with his daughter.

Lace walked into the room. She was puffing a fresh blunt of what smelled like reggie. The word family rang in her ear.

"We family but you with this bitch, and my momma cold in the ground. Yeah nigga... family." Diamond contemplated the current events as she stormed out the room.

"Diamond, you just do what I said girl, you understand me?!" her father yelled behind her.

She was at a crossroad and had to choose a path.

CHAPTER FIVE

Cupidite Luxure

Miller was captivated by the shimmer of the diamonds on the cross pendant in the glass jewelry case. His hands pressed against the glass leaving prints. The chime of other customers entering and exiting the store echoed in the background. His left hand began to itch. Miller dug his hands into his pockets. The lint from his pockets went under his nails. The realization he didn't have a dollar soon set in. He knew there was no way he could buy it. Rage grew inside him. Miller was fed up with being broke. He walked out of the jewelry store empty handed and pissed.

Miller knew he needed to come up with a plan and quick. Being broke was not his style. This is not the life he was meant to live. He was supposed to have fancy cars, houses, and a flock of hoes.

"I see you have an eye for fine ice." said a stranger.

Miller looked up with a side eye. Standing at the bus stop was a strange looking man in a three-piece suit, smoking a cigar. His hair looked uncombed and as if it never saw water. His skin was brown and ashy. His teeth where long and yellow.

"What's your point?" Miller asked, annoyed.

The stranger smiled. "I can help you wit dat... all the finer things in life. Money, cars, and hoes."

Miller's interest was piqued. "How?"

The stranger smiled. "Get in mon ami... I explain everything." The strange man pointed at a brand new black jaguar. The sun danced on the wet paint job.

Without hesitation Miller jumped in. The car smelled of new leather. The growl of the motor turned Miller on. He had to have one. After a few blocks Miller had the strange man take him to an apartment where he often chilled.

A tall, curvy, young eight-month pregnant girl opened the door. Despite her growing belly, she wore a halter top and panties.

"Go in the back room while we talk." Miller commanded.

He grabbed her ass as she left the room. The two gentlemen sat on the white leather sofa in the living room. The stranger pulled the glass coffee table closer. He pushed the jet magazines to the side. The stranger placed a plastic bag filled with white powder on the table.

"Is that...?" He dipped the tip of his finger in the bag and took a taste. He regretted it instantly.

The stranger grins. "Baking soda."

Miller sat back, confused and becoming angrier by the second. "Yo man, don't be wasting my time playing games." The stranger laughed as he stood and motioned for him to follow him.

"We go in da kitchen and I show you magic!" A grin crawled across the stranger's ashy face.

"I can turn that baking soda into white gold!" The stranger took a small pot from the dishrack and filled it with hot water. He set it on the stove and turned the fire up high.

"If you trying to make some crack, you late. Everybody knows how to cook that shit." Miller said, growing more and more agitated.

"White gold, mon ami, white gold!" The stranger said, still grinning like a Cheshire cat.

The stranger poured the baking soda into the boiling water. He watched silently for a second as foam began to appear. He then pulled a small vial of what appeared to be gold glitter from his pants pocket.

Miller laughed. "You gonna bedazzle the baking soda nigga? What the fuck?!"

The stranger grabbed a teaspoon and poured the glitter in it.

"Just a touch!" He said excitedly. He then stirred the concoction three time and turned the fire off. "White gold!"

Miller peeked into the pot and couldn't believe his eyes, it was full of white powder. "The shit looks legit!"

The stranger then dumped the contents of the pot into a Ziploc bag. He dipped his long bony finger in the bag. Inside his long brown pinky nail was the white substance.

"Try this."

Miller reluctantly, yet curiously took a bump from the stranger's finger. He immediately felt a surge run through his body. It was the best bump he's ever taken.

"Holy shit! That's ...."

The stranger laughed. "Pure booger sugar baby!"

Without hesitation Miller wanted in. "What I gotta do?"

"I will give you an endless supply of this. You will be the plug and the connect. You can take over the streets. They will have to come to you. Think about it... You can buy anything you want... you can have whoever you want. All the power and respect will be yours! In exchange for what I give you, you give me souls."

"Souls? What you mean?"

"Exactly what I said mon ami. I serve you in this life, you serve me in the afterlife." The stranger glared at him, his mischievous smile was replaced with a sinister gaze. His eyes glowed a fiery red for a brief second.

There was no doubt in Miller's mind that this man was not of this world. His greed clouded his better judgement. Miller wanted the world, and this was his chance to cash in. He was eager to give the stranger whatever he wanted. "Yes, you can have mine!"

With a devilish grin the stranger said, "We already have yours... I need your first born."

Miller laughed to himself. It was a girl and he wasn't that fond of the idea of having a daughter anyway.

Miller locked eyes with the stranger "Bet!"

The stranger laughed again. "What is it for a man to have his soul with no profits? All you have to do is sign this paper and we start tonight." The stranger pricked the tip of Miller's index finger. Miller signed his name in his own blood. The deal was made and sealed.

Like clockwork, over the next twenty years, Miller and the stranger met once a week to trade product for souls. He had every block on smash. The young boys couldn't resist the call of the streets. They would see Miller pull up in nice cars, fancy clothes, jewelry and they wanted in, just as he had when he met the stranger. He had more women then he could count. They all wanted to live like the rappers on t.v. Miller hardly lifted a finger. Everyone had to come to him if they wanted to eat. Miller was able to supply the stranger with ten to fifteen names a week.

* * *

The rubies on his pinky ring caught the light off the lamp as he rolled another joint waiting for his top runner, King. He brought more money than Miller could count. Miller loved it. When King started to eye his daughter Diamond, Miller had no issue. Diamond was built like her mother, tall and slender, with full lips and hips. Miller knew King was fucking the shit out of her, but he would do anything to keep his top runner happy.

One day, as Miller sat at his desk counting money, the stranger burst through the door with fire in his eyes, breathing heavily.

"You introduced Diamond to the animal, now she pregnant! You promised her to me!"

"Shit, she is?" Miller had no clue his daughter was pregnant.

"He touched her!" the stranger started to pace the floor. "The deal is off."

Miller stood knocking some of the money to the floor. "Hold up... you can have her!"

"No, no, he touched her!" The stranger yelled, still frantically pacing the floor.

"You can have her, the baby and King...He loves money more than me!" Miller pleaded. He couldn't lose his supply.

The stranger stopped pacing and smiled. "Even better." He rubbed his hands together.

Miller picked up the phone and called King and Diamond for a meeting. They arrived an hour later.

"Miller, we need to talk to you." King started the conversation, thinking he knew what the meeting was about.

"You got my daughter pregnant...I know...We here to talk business."

Diamond and King looked at each other, shocked that he knew.

Miller walked toward the stranger standing in the corner. "This is my silent partner, as you know, no names needed. Just hear him out."

Diamond was all ears. She never heard the stranger speak. He was just always there, as long as she could remember. Her mother was leery of him and warned her never to speak to her father's silent partner. She obeyed.

"King I got a proposition." The stranger said as he emerged from the shadows. "I got more product than I can move. I need help to branch out... I want you to go into business with me."

"How much we talking?" King asked.

The stranger smiled. "More money than you can imagine. Kingpin status. My fee is small considering what I have to offer. I'm the plug and the supplier. I can help you get whatever. Bitches will be throwing pussy at you! My fee ... souls." He began to drool.

"Souls?!" King and Diamond said in unison.

"Yes" the stranger hissed.

"What the hell you talking about?" King asked, thinking the stranger had to be joking.

"Don't be a bitch! You know you want power and money! Take the deal." The stranger's nails dug into King's shoulder.

King slammed to stranger against the wall. A thin cloud of dust escaped from his dingy suit.

"I am one of the siete deadly. She was promised to me before she was born. Until my name is uttered she's mine!" The stranger glared and pointed in Diamond's direction.

"Daddy, what the fuck is he talking about?" Diamond looked at her father, and she knew by the look on his face that the stranger spoke the truth. "You sold me?"

Miller looked at his daughter without a hint of emotion. "You lived a good life, didn't you?"

"You don't own her!" King growled.

Diamond rushed up to King. "You have to guess his name. My father sold my soul!"

"You believe this shit?" King asked puzzled.

"Yeah, I do. My mother used to always say she thought my daddy sold his soul to the devil, I thought she was off some other shit!" Diamond grabbed Kings arm as they both slowly backed away from the stranger.

"He said, siete deadly. That's Spanish! Seven deadly sins. One of them is his name!" she realized.

"Sloth!" King yelled. The stranger chuckled lightly. "Murder!" he called out. The stranger laughed a bit louder. Greed!?" The stranger's laughter abruptly stopped. His eyes grew large, fear was written on his face.

"Try in Spanish!" Diamond yelled.

"Codicia! Greed!" King hollered out.

Smoke started to rise from his clothes. Codicia started stomping and yelling. His stomps sounded like bombs going off. He stomped so hard he fell through the floor leaving a pile of smoldering clothes.

King turned and walked to Miller.

Diamond wasn't religious, but she did a couple of signs of the cross after witnessing such an unbelievable thing.

"The devil was in my house. Right here with us all these years, and you let him in? My mother was right all these years, and you acted like she was crazy?" Tears streamed down her face. She was in shock from what she'd just seen.

"You really thought I would sell my soul for this shit?! You sold your own daughters soul? For this?! Man, you can have this shit. I promise you'll never see Diamond again!"

King grabbed Diamond by the hand and rushed her out of the house. He realized he'd just looked true greed, the devil himself, in the eye and almost lost it all.

CHAPTER SIX

Fake Is The New Real

Doc sat back on his bunk in his cell. His mind started to drift. He couldn't believe he had been set up. There was no way he was taking the fall. He had worked too hard to go out like that. He was building an empire, and there was no way in hell King was going to take it.

Doc decided to call Keyonnia.

"Hey baby." He said after she accepted his call. Doc tried to keep his cool. "Is there anything you need to tell me?"

"What you talkin' bout?" she asked.

"I saw the pic's Kiki. You givin' dat nigga King head!"

"It wasn't even like dat!" she whined.

Keyonnia's mind started to race. She had to come up with something. How did Doc see the pic? He's in jail. One word popped into her head.... Diamond. Diamond was jealous and setting her up. Lace was right.

"Look Kiki, I need you to look out for me. I got some money stashed at the spot in a box under the floor in my room." Keyonnia cut him off.

"Dat's gone, King Moved to another spot, Diamond talked him into it."

Doc needed that money. He needed a lawyer.

"Look Kiki, I need you to get me a lawyer." he told her.

"I got you baby. Don't worry, I'll get the money some kinda way." She assured him.

The time on the phone ran out. Doc went back to his cell. He had to put all his trust in Keyonnia. His home boy flipped on him and his money was gone. He paced the small cell trying to keep his cool.

* * *

Keyonnia dropped her cell phone and ran into the bathroom where she found her sister Miesha plucking the hair from her chin and neck.

"Bitch! I got a lick!" she said excitedly.

"What you talking about." Miesha asked as she pulled a hair from her chin.

"Doc called me and told me to get his money to get a lawyer."

"Say what!" Miesha turned to look at her sister.

"Yea…. I told him it was gone." She said with a sly smile.

"Shit! You think it's still there?"

"Gotta be."

The girls ran to the motel room next door and grabbed their grandma's keys. They didn't give Margaret time to respond before taking her car.

"Girl… you think it's still there?" Miesha lit up with excitement.

"I hope… I need some money!"

"I want an apartment."

"Girl you stupid… you betta wait on dat government assistance to kick in." Keyonnia told her.

"I'm tired of dat motel! Ricky is doing way too much. He got me doing my work and everybody else work too. He taking full advantage of my situation." Miesha was getting frustrated.

"We won't be on the waiting list long. Plus you should be pushing up on Ricky, he got dat bread. He owns like four or five motels from what I heard." She suggested.

Keyonnia and Miesha parked in front of Doc's old trap spot. Miesha looks both ways then asked, "You think the police watching?"

Keyonnia sucked her teeth. "It's been two months, ain't no way they still watching. You comin'?"

Miesha was too nervous to go in. "I'll keep watch."

"More money for me." Keyonnia said under her breath as she walked toward the house.

Deep down Miesha knew her sister was a snake, and she had a bad feeling about walking into that house. She would take the "L", besides she could simply take from her sisters not so secret stash.

The trapped summer heat in the house hit Keyonnia in the face when she opened the door. The air was stale and uncomfortable. She went to the backroom where she used to fuck Doc. She got on her knees searching for an opening.

"Bam! Gottem!" She lifted the panel and found 4 duffel bags. She pulled each out and opened them.

"Bands will make her dance!" she started to dance around the room. She quickly checked the rest of the house to see what was left before grabbing the bags and running to the car. She tapped the trunk and Miesha pushed the button to pop it open. Soon as Keyonnia sat in the passenger seat, Miesha couldn't wait to ask.

"How much?!"

"It was two bags... not much, but enough for me to go shopping." She lied.

"So, we each get a bag?" Miesha was eager to spend.

"No, I'll give you some but I earned dat! I sucked his sweaty ass balls *and* blew in his ass to get dat cash!" Miesha knew her sister was lying. She always got extra when she was covering her ass.

Margaret was waiting outside the motel when they arrived. She didn't even let Miesha park the car. She hopped in and pulled off as Keyonnia pulled the last duffle bag out the car.

"Bitch!" Keyonnia mumbled as she walked back to the room.

Margaret was sick and tired of dealing with the girls. She jumped in the car and reflected on the circumstances that put them in her care. She and Wolf had been good friends with their mama, but she was dead and gone. Margaret was ready to cut to cut the strings. They had worn out their welcome. They were truly not her responsibility. Hell, they were not even her flesh and blood. This was Wolf's family, his stable, and her loyalty to him was over. She was too old to be anyone's bottom bitch, let alone a dead mans. Living in a motel was beneath Margaret. Phoenix threw her off her game, but pay back had to wait until Margaret got on her feet. She pulled out her cell phone and made a phone call she really didn't want to make.

A hunky voice on the other end answered. "What's up?"

"I need to see you."

"Meet me at the office at 5pm." Click.

Margaret felt she had one last try to get and stay on top. She started out young being addicted to nice things. She was determined to end her life the same. Whatever the cost.

* * *

Doc could feel the walls closing in on him. He had to get out. His work was gone, his stash was gone, and his right-hand man was fucking his girl. Keyonnia was playing it cool, but Doc knew she was fucking King. Fuck, he didn't know what to tell Miller about the dope the police took, now he had a price on his head. Doc had to come up with plan, but he needed outside help. He went to use the phone during rec time. Before her could dial a number, he felt something sharp in his side.

"Word on the streets is you got a story to tell. I got a warning for you... yo name pop up on some paperwork, it's gone popup on a tombstone too." A deep voice whispered in his ear.

"What the fuck you talking about?!"

"Nigga don't play stupid... Miller got everything on lock, and ears everywhere. Ya feel me!" He poked Doc in the side with the sharp object just enough to let him know he meant business.

"Lay down or get buried nigga!" The huge muscular man gave Doc an icy glare before walking off.

"Fuck!" Doc thought. He had already given a partial statement. He had to come up with something quick. The DA wanted another statement, and soon. Doc had two choose to either snitch and get killed, or spend the rest of his life in prison. He knew he was not built for that jail life. Doc gave up his place in line for the phone. He walked to his cell and plopped down on his bunk. He had to brainstorm.

* * *

Miesha stepped out of the shower and walked in

on Keyonnia talking on the phone.

"Come here... I got somebody dat want to say hey." She motioned for her.

"Who?!"

"Just get da phone."

Miesha placed the phone to her ear. The color ran from her face, and her hands began to shake as the familiar deep voice on the phone spoke.

"Oh... you can't speak?... Don't act like dat. Ha! Ha!" Keyonnia teased.

Miesha hung up the phone as tears ran down her face. She glared at her sister.

"You joking... right?!" She managed to say after a long pause.

"What!" Keyonnia laid back on the bed and popped her tongue.

"You know that nigga use to rape me and Phoenix when we were little... Tell me you not fuckin' wit him!" Miesha was pissed off at this point. She knew her sister was heartless and selfish, but some shit you just don't do.

"Damn bitch, dat was in the past. Shit, he said yo pussy was wet like you liked it anyway."

Miesha grabbed the empty ice bucket on the table and cracked Keyonnia across the head. She bounced off the bed and hit the floor, knocked out cold. Miesha finished putting on her clothes. She grabbed one of the two duffel bags of money. She knew there was more hidden somewhere, but she only took what she felt she deserved. Miesha left the motel, and her sister, and vowed never to look back again.

* * *

Margaret walked into the office with full confidence. It had been a while, but she still had game. The young receptionist ignored her presence. Margaret cleared her throat and spoke.

"I am here to see J... Mr. Hollingsworth please." the young woman made no effort to make eye contact.

"Please have a seat." She said dryly, never taking her eyes from her computer screen.

After thirty minutes, Margaret's patience level was very low.

"He will see you now." The dry receptionist informed her.

Margaret's heart began to race. She stood, took a deep breath, and walked into the large corner office.

"Have a seat. If my memory serves me correctly, I believe you like two cubes of ice in your scotch?"

"Yes please."

The gentleman brought Margaret a glass and sat on the corner of his desk.

"So, what's the reason for this urgent visit?" He asked, staring directly into her eyes.

Margaret took a sip from her glass.

"I need an apartment." She blurted out.

"And I factor into this how?" He asked, sounding genuinely confused.

"Jeffrey, let's not play games. I hate to beg."

"Mmm but you have always looked good on your knees." Jeffrey said as a huge grin grew across his face.

Margaret became flustered...no one had talked to her like that in years.

"Look, you know I need your ass! You ain't seen me in years. I'm here asking, what more do I have to do?"

"Red, things aren't like they use to be."

"You are the Major, you have ways."

"Red, this is not the old days any more. Our old street ranks don't matter."

"Now Jeffery... we both know you can help me."

"Red everything is accounted for here. This business is as legit as they come. Missing money traces back to me? Hey, accounting will blow the whistle loud as shit! I can't afford a scandal."

Margaret grinned and placed her glass of scotch on the table. She scooted to the edge of her chair. "I would hate for your wife and your beloved city to know your panty size and your sweet tooth for chocolate dicks."

Jeffery's already pale face turned beet red. Before he could walk away Margret grabbed his belt. She unzipped his pants and began to massage his manhood.

"Now tell me you can't help me." His eyes closed and he began to moan. "Now, tell me you *will* help me."

She slid his shaft into her mouth and stroked him with her tongue. He loved to see his milky white skin against her deep chocolate. The sight of it excited him even more. He exploded in her mouth. She stood up and wiped her lips.

"You have until Friday to find me a place, don't try to call my bluff Jeff. I ain't got shit to lose these days." she said calmly and walked out the door.

***

Keyonnia woke up on the floor with a massive headache. She couldn't believe Miesha got jealous and hit her.

"Fake bitch!" She went to check on the money she'd hidden from Miesha it was still there, minus one bag. She was pissed off., but relieved her sister didn't rob her blind. She had to get out of that motel and find something to get high on. She called Lace.

"Yo, can I come see you?" she asked, her voice full of attitude.

"What the hell crawled up your ass?"

"I'll tell you when I get there." She responded.

"Come on then." Click.

Keyonnia paced side to side while she waited on Lace to come out front with some coke. Diamond and King pulled up in front of the house. Diamond exited the vehicle first.

"Must be eating good. You getting fat!" she said to Diamond sarcastically.

Diamond looked in her direction.

"I'm eating good as shit now that I'm pregnant!" Diamond told her, intending to make her jealous.

"Who put it there?" Keyonnia asked as Lace stepped outside and handed her a vial.

"Kiki, you know damn well this is King's baby." Diamond said as she rubbed her stomach. "Stop playing with yourself!"

Keyonnia placed some powder on her pointer finger and sniffed it off. She sucked the remaining residue clean.

"Ugh!" Diamond said disgusted as King silently walked up behind her before they walked into the house.

Lace and Kiki sat outside of the house for a while taking bump after bump and chain smoking Newport's.

"I swear dat bitch get under my skin!" Lace proceeded to light another cigarette. "Look at dat shit. He walked up like you wasn't even here. Dat bitch got him not speaking to you!"

Before Keyonnia could reply, King and Diamond busted through the door with Miller in pursuit.

King yelled at Miller. "Fuck dat devil shit man! I'm done and my lady done too!"

Keyonnia watched as King placed his hand on Diamond's four-month baby bump. Her ears began to ring. She could only see their mouths moving, she couldn't hear any words. She felt herself leave her body. It was as if her soul floated above her body by some uncontrollable force. In horror, she saw herself push King to the side and pull out her blade. Keyonnia watched helplessly as she stabbed Diamond repeatedly in the stomach. Blood began to splash and she saw a red river run down Diamonds legs as she bent over in pain. King shoved Keyonnia out of the way as Diamond pushed uncontrollably, and her partially developed baby hit the pavement.

Dread swept over Keyonnia. Why couldn't she stop? She felt a rush of wind as she was thrown back into her body. Miller body slammed her to the pavement. She locked eyes with Lace and read her lips say, "Thank you". The ringing in her ears subsided and she could now hear Diamond's screams as she held her dead baby. Keyonnia tried to say sorry as Miller's fist connected with her jaw. The thunderous force caused her head to hit the pavement with a sickening thud, and she blacked out.

CHAPTER SEVEN

Karma Never Sleeps

Keyonnia woke to a throbbing pain on the side of her head. It was hard to breathe through her nose. She felt sharp pains in her ribs as she tried to take a deep breath. The lights in the room started to hurt the one eye she could open. She attempted to cover her face but she couldn't move.

"What the fuck". Keyonnia mumbled through heavily swollen lips.

"You're restrained to the bed." A voice boomed in her ear.

Keyonnia jumped at the sound of the deep male voice.

"I'm Detective Kegel." The voice boomed again.

Keyonnia groaned, then rested back onto the pillow. "Where am I?"

"You're in the hospital and we need to ask you some questions." The detective stated.

"I ain't saying shit without my grandma." She groaned again. Her jaw was stiff and swollen.

"Well you have no choice. She is in ICU, she had a stroke." He said with no emotion.

"You're lying!" She scoffed.

Keyonnia tried to pull her arm from the straps.

"Ma'am you need to calm down!" The detective instructed.

"Man, if she don't want to help me just say it! Don't lie about her being sick." Keyonnia fired back.

"Ma'am, do you understand? She had a stroke" The detective spoke slowly.

"She's turning her back on me like everybody else. It's cool... I got me." Keyonnia choked back tears.

He quickly changed the subject.

"I need to know what happened yesterday." His emotionless eyes fixated on her face.

"What you mean? Anybody can tell you dat bitch attacked me!" Keyonnia tried to yell, but instead mumbled due to her severely injured jaw.

"So how did this come about?" He probed.

"Dat bitch trifling! I stabbed her cause she provoked me! Dat bitch a broke ass gold digger...

she was fuckin' wit Doc because he was the plug and had money. He got popped and to fuck wit me cause she jealous, she started going at King." Keyonnia spat.

"What were you doing at the scene?"

"I went to cop some blow from my home girl Lacy, and dat bitch Diamond just popped up fuckin' wit me! The last straw was her faking like she pregnant and all over my man in my face. She made me do it... hell, all I did was slash her face! Dat bitch will be aight." Keyonnia laughed. She sucked her teeth and turned her head away from him. The fact she felt justified was written all over her face.

"Well ma'am I'm here to tell you, the victim was not faking. In fact, you stabbed her repeatedly until she miscarried. The baby died." He stated.

"You lying! Dat bitch wasn't pregnant and she ain't no victim. I am!" Keyonnia was pissed at the thought. She tried to pick her mind for any memories of what the detective accused her of, she found none. "I just sliced her face, I ain't kill no baby!"

Keyonnia became silent and faced the wall. Her eyes became distant and her face was expressionless.

"Hello... Ma'am?" He tried to get her attention.

No response. She hadn't blinked and her breathing slowed. The detective's partner looked at him with skepticism on his face. He walked to the bed and tapped her.

"Who are you?" Keyonnia questioned.

"Ma'am we don't have time for games." Detective Kegel said impatiently.

"Man, I don't know you!" Keyonnia spat back.

"You just gave us a statement." the detective stated.

"Man, I just woke up!" Keyonnia slurred.

"Excuse me, detectives?" Dr. Nick Carson walked into the room. "This woman is my patient. She has not been cleared to give any statements."

Detective Washington closed his notepad. "Fine... we're done here."

Keyonnia looked the doctor up and down, from head to toe.

"I'm Dr. Nick Carson." he stated.

Keyonnia stared at him with a blank expression.

"I believe you blacked out when you assaulted the young lady." the doctor suggested.

Keyonnia rolled her eyes.

"I have your medical history."

"What da fuck do you want?" Keyonnia snapped.

"To help you." the doctor sounded concerned.

"Man get the fuck out the room... better yet untie me so I can move. I can't feel my hands." Keyonnia hissed.

"We can untie the restraints, but you need to promise you won't leave."

"Whatever man... untie me please! My ass itchin'!" Keyonnia ordered.

The doctor unstrapped her arms.

"Thank you." Keyonnia said softly.

Wham! She punched the doctor in the face knocking him to the floor. She jumped from the bed and started to run down the hall. The doctor ran to the door holding his jaw.

"Stop her!"

A nurse reached for her by grabbing her hospital gown. Keyonnia slipped out of it and continued to run down the hallway naked. A male orderly stuck out his arm and closed lined her. Keyonnia fell backwards slamming her head on the floor. She was knocked out cold.

Dr. Nick walked up to Keyonnia. "Take her to the psych ward. Strap her down good." the doctor commanded grabbed his jaw in pain.

* * *

"Thank you for coming Miss. Graham." the young woman and the doctor shook hands.

"Please have a seat" the doctor suggested.

"What is this about?" Miesha asked.

"Well as you know your sister has been here six months and has a pending court case for attempted murder and murder of an unborn child." The doctor explained.

"And you called me because?" Miesha asked.

"Miss Graham, your sister needs help..." the doctor started to speak.

"I know..." Miesha spoke very dryly.

"I mean she needs legal and physical help. She will need a caretaker." the doctor pleaded.

"Not my problem."

"With your grandmother being in the nursing home after her severe stroke, you are the next of kin. She's your sister. She's your responsibility." the doctor was confused.

Miesha stood and placed a black bag on the doctor's desk. "I will only state this once. That narcissistic bitch is not my responsibility... in this bag is $20,000.00. Forget you contacted me." Miesha barked.

She turned and stormed out the door. She was done with Keyonnia. Her sister was pure evil and she wanted no parts of it. Miesha didn't even touch much of the money she took from her. She held on to it, afraid that the police would find out she had Doc's money somehow. It turned out to be the best decision she could make. Now that she'd given the doctor some hush money, she could wash her hands clean of her mentally disturbed sister forever.

The doctor sat looking at the bag on his desk, almost afraid to look inside. He knew greed would take over and win. After 30 minutes he opened the bag, and indeed there was a pile of money inside. He placed the bag in his desk and locked it. Dr. Carson marked Keyonnia's file as abandoned and ward of the state, due to no next of kin.

* * *

Dr. Carson made his usual 3 o'clock stop into Keyonnia's room. "How is she nurse?" he asked

"The same. The meds have her sedated. We tried last week to let her walk around and she broke a nurse's nose and had sex with a male patient." the nurse stated.

"She's a handful!" the doctor joked.

"Yes, well I'm about to make my rounds. Do you need anything doctor?" the nurse asked.

"No... I'm fine." the doctor stated.

The nurse left the room leaving the doctor alone with Keyonnia.

"Hello, sleeping beauty." he whispered in Keyonnia's ear. He kissed her softly on the lips and pulled back the covers. He slid his hand up her inner thigh. He unbuttoned his pants with his other hand.

Knock Knock

Dr. Carson quickly fixed his clothes and covered her back up. Detectives Kegel and Washington walked into the room.

"How can I help you gentlemen?" the doctor asked.

"We came to see if she was ready to face trial." stated Detective Kegel.

"I have filed my papers. She cannot face trial as she is not mentally competent." the doctor said.

"So, you're helping her walk!" huffed Detective Washington.

"I am doing what's right, she can't be held accountable due to her instability." Dr. Carson explained.

The detective smirked and left the room. The doctor went back to Keyonnia, removed her sheets and pulled off his pants.

"Where were we sleeping beauty?"

Five months after Dr. Carson filed his paperwork, the court found Keyonnia unfit to stand trial and face charges. One day not long after that, nurse Krystal rushed into his office.

"Dr. Carson I think we have a problem." the nurse blurted out.

"What's wrong?" Dr. Carson stood from his desk.

"We thought the patient was swollen from a buildup of gas..." the nurse trailed off. "She's pregnant!" the nurse said.

"Who!" Dr. Carson yelled.

"Keyonnia Graham... she may be 5 or 6 months." the nurse explained.

"Are you sure?" the doctor questioned her.

"I felt it move." the nurse stated.

"Order an ultrasound, now!" the doctor ordered.

Dr. Cason's heart began to race as the ultrasound revealed not one, but two heart beats.

"Dr. Carson what are we going to do?" nurse Krystal asked.

"Have any male patients roamed the hall?" the doctor asked trying to throw the blame in any direction other than his.

"Yes, and there were the few times we let her out." the nurse admitted.

"We have to wean her off the meds. We can't keep her sedated now that she is pregnant." He sighed.

Dr. Carson went back to his office. His mind was all over the place.

He and his wife couldn't have children, and the crazy sleeping beauty was carrying his twins. He was filled with mixed emotions. On one hand, he had a failing marriage, and in the other, a few moments of lust produced twins. If anyone knew they were his, he would lose his career and his life. He'd surely be prosecuted.

Keyonnia was weaned off the meds slowly. Dr. Nick still made his daily 3pm visits.

"So, when do you release me and move me into the house?" Keyonnia asked out if the blue after he'd had his way with her for the umpteenth time.

Startled, the doctor dropped his clipboard. "Excuse me?"

"Just because I didn't move or talk doesn't mean I couldn't hear." Keyonnia laughed. A smirk crawled across her face. "I heard every word, how beautiful I was, how I made your dick hard. I even heard when you said my pussy was better than your wife's!" Keyonnia's words dripped with poison.

His expression changed, beads of sweat popped on Dr. Carson's forehead.

"Now we both know you put these babies in me while I was sleeping. Now you either get me out of here and set me up nice, or I'm telling yo wife!" Keyonnia hissed

"You're a vindictive bitch, aren't you?" the doctor snapped.

"And you're a short dick motherfucker, aren't you?! Besides you have my file, don't act surprised." Keyonnia laughed again.

"Give me time to think. This is a lot. I can't just snap my fingers and get you out of here."

He said, frustrated.

"I don't give a damn what you gotta do, but you're gettin' my ass outta here!" Keyonnia yelled.

Dr. Carson looked at her growing belly. He had to come up with a plan and fast.

It took Dr. Carson three months to push the paperwork to get Keyonnia released. The harder part was getting the new house without his wife seeing their savings account ravaged. To be with Keyonnia while she delivered, Nick told his wife he had a convention and an off-site assignment that would take 8 weeks. She always believed everything he said.

"Yo wife dumb as fuck...aint no way I would believe no bullshit like that." Keyonnia joked.

"Come on... it's her money helping to pay for all this." Nick explained.

"Mmm... tell her thanks." Keyonnia hummed. She kicked back on the sofa. "Malaysia's diaper needs to be changed." Keyonnia pointed out.

"Why can't you change her diaper? I'm not here to be a nanny, we got to share the responsibility Kiki." He complained.

"You'll bring your ass here every day and night when I call!" Keyonnia ordered. "Your sleeping beauty is wide awake now!" She pointed her freshly manicured finger at the baby and turned the volume up on the Future video she was watching.

Ring Ring

"Answer that phone nigga and I'll flip!" Keyonnia snapped.

"It's my wife." Nick pleaded.

Keyonnia threw her soda at his head. "Nigga don't try me!" Keyonnia screamed.

Nick let the call go to voicemail.

* * *

Two years dragged by for Nick. Keyonnia gave him pure hell. His kids made it all worth it.

"I don't know how I will tell my wife about you and the twins." Nick told her.

"Do you love me?" Keyonnia asked.

"Yes!" he answered truthfully.

"Do you love your kids?"

"That's stupid to ask."

"Well tell the bitch before I do!" Keyonnia ordered.

"Please calm down. It's not that easy!" Nick pleaded.

"Fuck dat shit... get out!" Keyonnia yelled.

"Kiki..."

"Get out!" she yelled again.

Her voice was filled with rage and her body shook. Nick lowered his head and walked out the door. Keyonnia slammed it behind him.

"I got something for his ass!" Keyonnia grabbed the twins and hopped into her car.

Bam Bam Bam

"Who is it?" A small voice behind the door called out.

Bam Bam Bam

"Who is it?" the voice called again.

"Nick's baby momma!" Keyonnia yelled.

"Excuse me?" The soft voice on the other side of the door sounded confused.

"Open the door bitch and find out!" Keyonnia snapped.

The door slowly opened. A small petite dark-skinned woman stood in the door. Keyonnia pushed the 2-year-old twins in her face.

"Since Nick ain't got the balls to tell you, I thought I would. We fuckin' and these his kids. I know you can't have none and he didn't know how to tell you. So now you know!"

Keyonnia yanked the twins by their arms and dragged them back to the car. She had a huge grin of satisfaction on her face.

Nick raced to Keyonnia's house and kicked the

door in. Keyonnia didn't budge from the couch. She sat there with a satisfied smirk on her face.

"What the fuck is wrong with you!"

"I told you to do it." She teased.

"What the fuck! AAAH! You're a crazy bitch!" he yelled in frustration as he stood in front of her.

"Yeah, and you like it!" Keyonnia grabbed his dick and put her tongue in his mouth. Nick gave in. She might be crazy, but her pussy was amazing. With cum dripping from her face, she told him, "You can never leave me alone."

Nick felt she was right. He had an unbearable weakness for her.

"Call out of work tomorrow and take me out."

"Kiki, I can't..." He trailed off.

She grabbed his dick again, stroking it as she looked deeply into his eyes.

"Ok...Ok." he gave in.

Keyonnia and Nick left the twins with a baby sitter.

"So... where to?" Nick asked.

"I want to go shopping." She stated.

"I just took you shopping."

"What's your point?! I said take me shopping!"

She dragged him around town for six hours

running in and out of boutiques. She was seriously draining his credit cards. They were on their way back home when Keyonnia's phone went off.

Buzz

She received a text.

Your aunt paid me so I went home.

"What the fuck?"

"What's wrong?" Nick asked.

"The babysitter said my aunt paid her?"

"Well, we are about to pull up."

Nick knew that white SUV anywhere. It was his wife's Land Rover.

"What's that in the driveway?" Keyonnia asked as they pulled in.

Horror stuck them both when they realized what the black masses were in the driveway.

"Nooo!" Keyonnia let out a scream that came from the pit of her soul. Her babies had been tied together with their own jump rope and ran over. Nick jumped out the car. His wife looked at him with swollen eyes full of tears and trails of black mascara streaming down her face.

'How could you! You knew I wanted children more than anything!" she screamed. "You went and found the most ghetto woman I've ever seen and you gave her children?!"

Nick tried to speak, but words would not escape his lips. Hot tears fell from his eyes. He looked over at the bloody mass of flesh that was once his beautiful twins.

"How could you...." he managed to say.

"Don't you lie to me. Don't you ever speak to me again!" He small voice was now a piercing shrill. "All these years Nick, and you ruined it

for ghetto trash."

Bang!

She shot him in the face at point blank range. He was dead before his body hit the ground.

His wife turned to Keyonnia with a dead look in her eyes. She was no longer in her body, something else took over, something sinister.

"You homewrecker, I hope it was all worth it." She said calmly as she raised the gun to her head.

Bang!

Keyonnia watched in what seemed to be slow motion, as tiny red pieces of flesh flew from the side of the woman's head. Theirs eyes locked. Blood streamed down the woman's face as she dropped to the pavement with a thud. Pieces of her brain hit Keyonnia's face.

She dropped to her knees and sat in the pool of her children's blood and gore. She screamed at the top her lungs over and over as she tried to put the twins shredded and busted bodies back together again. It was a grotesque puzzle she didn't have the answer to. Keyonnia heard sirens in the distance, she leaned over and picked up the gun Nick's wife dropped. As the sound of the sirens drew closer, Keyonnia put the gun to her head.

She looked down at her daughter's and let out an unearthly wail as she pulled the trigger.

CHAPTER EIGHT

Kill or Be Killed

"Bitch you fucking with my money! Where the fuck you get off refusing to suck a customer's dick?! You fuck and suck who the hell I tell you to!"

He backhanded Miesha, making her lose balance.

"Yes sir...I'm sorry...it smelled funny" Miesha was able to stutter before his pale white hand went across the other side of her face.

"Go clean some rooms and get the fuck out my face!" The motel manager ordered. Miesha took her cleaning chart and headed for the elevator.

The whole situation was horrible. She was trying to work off her debt and get the hell out of town. Miesha knew borrowing money from Rick had strings to it, but she needed it to keep Margaret in the nursing home. She had no idea he would sell her to a pimp's motel. She was trapped. He always had his people outside, so the women couldn't leave without him knowing. Miesha had only been there for a month, but it felt like a lifetime.

Once she was in the elevator alone, Miesha pulled out a small baggy containing white powder. She told herself only three bumps, that would get her through the day. She put rest of the powder back in her pocket.

When Miesha arrived at the first room she held her breath and opened the door. She let out a deep breath the room was empty which meant she only had to clean the room. She cleaned it and quickly moved on to the next room, praying that it was empty as well. Her heart began to race again as she slowly opened the door.

"Oh shit!" She gasped. She quickly put her hand over her mouth. Inside the room were three young girls, 12 or 13 years old at the most. One was tied to the bed. Once she met eyes with Miesha, she tried to scream through her gag. The other two were tied back to back on the floor. They begged with their eyes, with tear soaked faces for Miesha to help them.

"Look I'm already fucked up, and this ain't my business." Miesha closed the door behind her leaving the little girls to their doom.

"Ain't nobody ever help me. Shit, who the fuck I look like helping somebody." Miesha mumbled to herself as she took two more hits of the white powder in her pocket.

Feeling the effects of the "white girl", she pushed her cleaning cart against the wall. She needed to talk to Ricky, she didn't want to trick anymore to work off her debt. She figured there had to be another way. She took two more bumps then walked to the manager's office where Ricky had the safe open counting money.

"What the fuck do you want?" He asked with an attitude.

"I want out." she said trying to clean her nose.

"Bitch get back to work!" he brushed her off and continued to count money.

"I saw those littles girls in that room... Be a shame if someone reported you." She said with a cocky grin.

Ricky put down the money and walked toward her.

"I know you not threating me..." He laughed as he wrapped his hands around her neck. "Dead coked up whores can't talk!" His grip got tighter. Miesha eyes began to water as she gasped for air. He backed her against his desk and squeezed. He could feel her pulse racing in her neck. Miesha kicked her arms and legs trying to free herself. She began to look around the room trying to find something, anything to hit him with. With one hand around his wrist trying to loosen his grip, with her free hand she found a pen. She closed her eyes and started to stab until finally his grip was off her. Miesha opened her eyes to she'd stabbed Ricky in the eye and the pen was still in his throat as he dropped to his knees gasping for air. She quickly ran to the safe and grabbed the money.

Miesha couldn't believe her luck she was free and had money. She grabbed Ricky's keys to his car and ran for the door.

She looked around outside to make sure the manager and his friends were nowhere in sight in front of the tiny motel. She hopped into Rick's car and put the key in the ignition. Miesha started the engine, snapped in her seatbelt and adjusted the rearview mirror. She caught a glimpse of herself and had to grab the mirror again to make sure she wasn't crazy. She saw herself as a little girl. Memories of the pain and torment she felt as her uncle violated her filled her head.

She knew she should just drive off, she was free. They'd kill her if they saw what she did to Rick. All she could see was their little brown faces, eyes wide with fear, pleading for Miesha's help.

She searched the car for a gun. She knew Rick had to have one in there somewhere. She found a .45 under the passenger seat.

Miesha, the timid sister. The little sister who was always nervous and afraid, stepped out of the dead man's car and headed towards the elevator. She was going to get those babies out of that room. She entered the elevator, pushed the button for the top floor, and took the safety off the gun.

To be continued...

URBAN PULP FICTION

MEET THE AUTHOR

Phoenix James

Growing up in South Carolina, Phoenix James was a daydreamer spending many of her days lost in her own thoughts. She created her own worlds and Universes.

In these worlds, she could control everything. Every "shoulda" "coulda" "woulda" in life Phoenix played out with different outcomes the way she wanted them to be. Every heartache, embarrassing moment, and, let down was reversed with a twist.

Phoenix's books are a mixture of urban street literature with a dash of supernatural. Kingpins, dope boys and demon's world collided for an unexpected thrill. Readers will find themselves traveling to a new place and seeing things from a different and unique perspective.

When not writing Phoenix spends her time with her music mogul husband and her four children. Stay tuned because Phoenix James has more books up her sleeve!

Books by Phoenix James

Urban Pulp Fiction: The Queen Has Landed

Urban Pulp Fiction: The Saga Continues

Her Unfaithful Dream (coming soon)

Fool For That (coming soon)

Love Lust Infatuation (coming soon)

Taste Of Honey (coming soon)

Real Street B$tch (coming soon)

The Rules are Meant To Be Broke (coming soon)

Connect with the author:

Facebook: Author Phoenix James

Facebook group: From the Mind of Phoenix James
https://www.facebook.com/phoenixjamesbooks/

Twitter: https://twitter.com/PhoenixJames7

IG: https://www.instagram.com/phoenixjamesbooks/

Goodreads: https://www.goodreads.com/author/
show/13515077.Phoenix_James

Amazon Fan page: https://www.amazon.com/Phoenix-
James/e/B079P6CJD1/ref=dp_byline_cont_book_1

Bookbub: https://www.bookbub.com/profile/phoenix-
james

Email-phoeinxjamesbooks@gmail.com

Thank you for allowing me to share my world with you.

Coming Soon

King looked from his steak plate to find Mercedes staring at him.

"What?" King took a sip of his drink.

"You really had to talk to her in front of me?"

"What?...Come on...don't start dat shit!...It never bothered you before"

Mercedes just glared at him. She felt the tips of ears warming up as she got more pissed. "What if I started fucking somebody else?"

King put down his fork. "Bitch what the fuck you talking about?!"

"You heard me.... What if I got another nigga and started fucking him?" Mercedes rolled her neck, sat back and smirked.

"Why would you say some crazy shit like dat?" King flared his nostrils.

"You always talking to her in front of of me like you don't care how I fell"

"Hold on how you just gone start changing shit? We always kicked like this...how you just changing shit now?"

"King you know how I feel about you"

"I ain't never hide nothing from you...you knew what was up from the jump. Diamond my old lady. I'm not about to start lying to you about her to make you happy!" King pulled money from his pocket and paid the bill." If you want to fuck somebody else that's on you...just know I want stick my dick back in you!" King slammed the money on the table and walked out the restaurant to his car.

This was the dumb shit King did not have time for. As King crossed the parking lot he noticed two chicks posted up on a car close to his.

"Dang nigga! You too good to speak?" the dark caramel chick screamed out.

"He must be!" the Latin chick chimed in.

"No disrespect sweetheart" King strolled over.

"Did you just call my homegirl a bitch!"

"What the fuck!" King was caught off guard as a group of guys surrounded him. The girls continued to scream and curse him out.

"I don't know what the fuck is going on but these chicks tripping"

"Yo my nigga that's my sister you are disrespecting" The biggest nigga standing 6"5 approached King.

King stood his ground and sized the nigga up. Out the corner of his eye King could see 4 more niggas on each side closing in.

"I don't know what the fuck y'all trying to do but I ain't that nigga you want to fuck wit!"

The big dude spoke again. "This bitch as nigga thank he tough!"

"I don't know yo sister, she called me over trying to holla then changed up" King was eyeing the dude to take out first.

"Oh so you calling my sister a liar"

"Something ain't right" King spit at the dude feet.

"My sister got a nigga... why would she holla at you?" The big dude was now an inch from King's face.

King knew he was out numbered but he wasn't the type to let no nigga punk him. He would go down fighting or blasting.

"You might want to remind her my nigga cause she hollered at me. I don't chase my liquor or no bitch!" King started to second guess if he should pull his iron out or fight straight up. The odds were not good for either one. He could should shoot the biggest but next one if not all eight shooting, or he could punch the biggest and get his ass kicked by at least six or five niggas. King knew he could take at least three. Before King could react, a glass bottle crashed against the side of his head. Blood clouded his vision as King swung out blindly. A foot connected with Kings ribs sending him to his knees. King attempted to reach for his gun when another foot connected with his jaw. King spit out a mouthful of blood.

"Fuck you pussy ass nigga!" King slurred. A fist connected with the back of Kings head. He felt light headed but attempted to swing.

"Y'all had to gang me cause y'all know otherwise

I would fuck yall up!" King puffed out the words as blood ran from his mouth. A blow landed on his right ear busting his ear drum. It sent pain direct to King's brain, the following behind the pain was sharp ringing noise. King could feel himself sleeping. The world began to spin, and he didn't know what was up or down. King laid down on the pavement unable to try and fight back as the group of niggas continued to punch and kick him. Before blacking out he thought he heard a female voice scream his name. He thought it might be Mercedes, but his body was to weak to move. King gave up to the struggle and blacked out.

PHOENIX JAMES

URBAN PULP FICTION